Tortured Souls

A Samantha Franklin Novel

By Pete Alexander

Dark Days Press
P. O. Box 92072
Long Beach, California 90809

First Edition: October 2015
The characters and events in this book are fictitious. Any similarity to real persons, living or dead, is coincidental and not intended by the author.

ISBN: 978-0-996-78291-3

www.petealexandermurdermysteries.com

Special thanks to:

Joanna Branson. I have no doubt that when my sister asked you to talk to me about this idea, you cringed at the thought and asked yourself, "What fresh hell am I getting myself into?" Thank you for your guidance and for putting up with my weird phone calls.

Professor Emeritus Pamela Upton. You helped me understand what physiological response a human body would have when exposed to certain kinds of, well, *things*. And you didn't call the police on me. Always a plus.

Derek Madden. You helped me understand vivisection, the name behind what I was describing in my writing.

PM and my wife and children for listening to my crazed ideas (and also not calling the police on me) and helping me to refine them until they have become what lies before you here.

And to J Mac and HMM, my editors in addition to Joanna.

1

WEDNESDAY

Suzie Brookhurst sat down in her office chair and dialed up Jane Woodman's number. Certain that everyone else had gone home, she hit the speakerphone button.

"Suzie! I was just about to call you. So, how did it go?" Jane asked.

"What are you trying to do to me?" Suzie asked. "What did I do to piss you off so bad?"

"So, the good doctor's house closed escrow, I see," Jane said.

"Yeah, it did. But I'll tell you, if you ever set me up with a client like him again, I'll kill you! He was such a jackass! No, I take that back. To say he was a jackass is an insult to all the jackasses of the world. He was beyond a jackass. They haven't yet invented words sufficient enough to describe what a jackass he is!" Suzie ranted.

"Yeah, I know," Jane commiserated. "But keep in mind, you've only had to put up with him for the past five days. I've been showing him properties on a daily basis for nearly a month before he decided on that place. He had insisted on living out away from the city, 'In a rural setting.' We're in Los Angeles. Do you know how hard it is to find property that's located out of the city in 'a rural setting'? I mean, I'd take him to a property and before I could even get out of the car he'd tell me, 'No, I don't like it'. Once, he agreed to meet me at that place way out Malibu Canyon Drive. You know the one, about an hour's drive from here? We pulled up and he said that it was on the wrong side of the street!"

"Well, if you ever bring me a client like him again, I'll kill you myself. Friend or no friend. I don't need his kind of business."

"Sure Suzie. You say that now, but when that commission check hits your bank account, then let's here you complain."

"You know Jane, you can be such a bitch sometimes."

"Thank you. Thank you. I appreciate and accept any and all compliments."

"You're such a dork," Suzie said with a giggle. "Any plans for tonight?"

"Of course. We've got some plotting to do."

"What do you mean?"

"You said it yourself, didn't you? He treats everybody like shit, right?"

"Yeah, from what I've seen. Do you have something in mind?"

"I think it's time somebody taught the good doctor

what happens to certain people when they mess with certain other people, don't you agree?"

"Jane, what have you got in mind?"

"Just a little something that will remind, not just our doctor, but all the Blake Covington's of the world why it's a bad idea to mess with the people they feel are beneath them. A little something that he won't see coming. Something that's beyond anything he's ever experienced."

"Do you have a plan?" Suzie asked with excited caution.

"Actually I have several. The question is, which one would hurt him where it counts the most? But let's talk about it in person. We need to act fast."

"When do you want to get together?"

"If you're done there, I can meet you in an hour at the usual place. I want to act on this tonight."

"Okay, I'll see you there," Suzie said and hung up the phone. As she sat back, she thought about all the terrible things she and Jane could do to Doctor Blake Covington. "It's time you learned your lesson, Blake," she said aloud.

From inside the darkened supply room, Suzie's secretary Margie Rice gently closed the door. After the conversation she'd just heard, it would probably be a bad idea to let Ms. Brookhurst know that she'd been in there. What are you two up to? she thought.

Margie waited until she heard Suzie lock the front door and start up her car before she let herself breathe again.

Five minutes later she left the supply room. She briefly thought about calling the police, but then thought better of it. "It's not like she's going to kill him," she said to the room at large.

2

After leaving Capitol Escrow, Blake Covington decided to take a drive up to his new home. When he reached the 10 freeway, he turned on the stereo and listened as the ominous song played:

> *If I shot you in the head, would it make you dead?*
> *If I shot you in the leg, would it make you beg?*
> *If I shot you in the knee, would it make you plead?*
> *If I shot you in the back, would your heart attack?*
>
> *If I shot you in the arm, would you lose your charm?*
> *If I shot you in the chin, would you lose that grin?*
> *If I shot you in the heart, would you fall apart?*
> *If I shot you in the ear, would you finally hear?*
>
> *If I shot you in the head, would it make you dead?*
> *If I shot you in the head, would it make you dead?*
> *If I shot you in the head (BANG!) Now you're dead.*

The sun had gone out of the sky by the time Blake turned off of the road and onto his driveway, but the pink and purple hues that danced in the sky were magnificent as they stretched over the ocean below. He drove up the tree lined drive and eased the blue Bugatti up in front of the three car garage. He shut the engine off and took in the beauty of his domain as he let out a relaxed sigh.

This would forever be his home. He opened the door to the vehicle and moved his foot out onto the pavement. He looked up at the house and sheer terror hit him. Light was coming from inside of the house. A flickering light. The light of a fire.

He ran from the car, not even bothering to pull the keys from the ignition. He grabbed his cell phone and tried to call 9-1-1, but there was no signal out here. Damn it, he thought. He burst through the front door, not even registering that it should have been locked. He ran inside and came to a stop when he reached the great room. At the far end of the room, someone had built a roaring fire in the fireplace. Relief washed over him. It was quickly replaced with anger. "Who's here?" Blake shouted.

No one answered.

"I said who's here?" he shouted even louder.

Still, there was no answer.

As he walked around the room, he noticed that on the kitchen countertop, there was a silver ice bucket with a bottle inside. A single champagne glass was next to it. As he came nearer to the countertop, he could see a hand written note. When he got within arm's reach of the note, he picked it up and read, "*Congratulations on the house· Enjoy the champagne!*"

He pulled the bottle from the ice. It was Dom Perignon.

Amateurs, Blake thought. Dom Perignon was what the working class drink when they want to feel above their station. Obviously, either Suzie or Jane were trying to suck up to him. Nice try ladies, but you're showing your lack of pedigree again. Still, it would be a shame to let this bottle go to waste, he thought.

Blake popped the bottle open and poured himself a glass. He downed it in one gulp. The thought of his home being on fire had shaken him up more than he had realized. He poured himself a second glass, set the bottle down on the counter and took a more dignified sip. He started to wander through his home. His home . "This is all mine," he said aloud. He took another sip and moved from the kitchen back into the great room. As he entered the living room, he took yet another sip.

It was when he was headed for the study that he started to feel a headache coming on. Great, he thought. Just what I need. Maybe if I try to relax a bit I can keep it at bay, he thought as he started to rock his head from side to side while alternating his shoulders up and down.

He moved into the study, took another sip and headed for the big windows that overlook the ocean below. Wow, he thought. This is going to be a bad one. He rubbed his temples slowly and gently and then he took another sip.

He was pulling the glass away from his lips when he heard a long, slow, scraping sound, like the sound of metal being dragged against wood. Sharp metal against the mahogany paneling in the hall. Then, he heard a soft, gentle voice, just above a whisper, call out, "Blaaaake."

Blake's head was starting to spin. He shouted out, "Who's there?" His head began to pound. He took another sip, draining his glass and headed towards the hall. He cautiously peered out around the corner and saw no one. He let out a sigh of relief and stepped out into the hall. He had almost convinced himself that it had been his imagination when he saw, on the wall, at about chest height, a long scrape in the wood paneling. As realization was setting in, he heard it again. The sound of metal, sharp metal, scraping, digging into wood and that soft, gentle voice, barely audible, calling out from the kitchen. "Blaaaake," it said.

Blake's panic was palpable. His head was throbbing. The room was spinning. He was confused. He followed the sound of the scraping and the voice into the kitchen. There was no one there. He poured himself a third glass of champagne. He was about to take another sip of the champagne, when he saw a long scrape in the solid oak kitchen cabinet doors. His heart was beating fast and hard now. "Okay, Blake. Get a hold of yourself," he said as the sound of metal scraping in wood sounded again, this time from the great room. Then he heard the voice again. "Blaaaake," it called. Was there something familiar in the voice? He started to stagger into the great room.

When he entered the great room, he saw a second champagne glass, with deep red lipstick on it, on the mantle above the fireplace. Confusion, panic, fear and anger all swirled around Blake's throbbing head. The voice spoke again, but this time it came from just behind him. "Good evening, Blake," the voice said.

Blake spun around, trying to look tough, but only barely keeping upright. "Who are you and what are you doing in my house?" he yelled at the stranger.

"Don't tell me you don't remember me, Blake," the stranger said with a mirthless laugh. "I know that's a powerful drug in your champagne, but not enough for you not to be able to remember me."

"Yoooouuuu," Blake said with wide eyes, full of recognition, dropping his nearly full glass on the carpeted floor.

"I've been waiting for this day for a long time Blake. A very long time," the stranger said as Blake lost consciousness.

3

THURSDAY

Samantha Franklin was, in all likelihood, the only detective in the Los Angeles Police Department's Homicide Division not lamenting the change that had just been announced. According to Captain Erikson, beginning tomorrow, all detectives would be paired with new partners. Although she didn't mind her current partner, Jennifer Daniels, as a person, she always felt like she was having to train her. Now she was hopeful that her new partner would have some experience.

"Franklin!" Erikson shouted.

Sam pulled her head out of the clouds. "On my way," she said, heading to the captain's office.

"Come on in. I want you to meet your new partner."

Sam walked in and saw a tall, thin young man that looked as though he were no older than sixteen. "Where's my new partner?" she asked.

"You're looking at him. Say hello to Detective Richard Evans."

Sam's head spun around to do a double take. She began to walk an investigatory circle around the young man. With heavy sarcasm she said, "You're joking, right? He looks like he doesn't have a driver's license yet. Has he even started shaving? When did he go to the academy? When he was ten?"

"Actually, I graduated from the academy when I was twenty," Detective Evans said, stepping forward, proudly sticking out his chest. "Two years ago."

Sam spun on her heels glaring at the captain. "What the hell is this? He's a detective after two years? It took me eight years, EIGHT YEARS to make detective," she said, slamming her fist onto his desk. "And now you want to pair me with this joker?"

"Take it easy, Sam. Try and get a hold of yourself. The chief and I talked about it and we agreed that you are the best detective we've got. You've got the right mind set and you're a damn good trainer. We've been watching how you've been with Daniels. It wasn't by accident you were paired with her. We wanted to see what kind of leader and trainer you would be. With that in mind, you're going train Evans here."

"I don't have time to babysit Junior," she said, flipping her thumb backwards at her new partner.

"I am a detective, you know. I have all of the necessary training…" Junior began.

"Shut it!" she snapped at him, while spinning around to face him, making a closing motion with the fingers on her left hand. "You have book knowledge. You don't know squat about the streets."

17

"Sam," Erikson said. "This comes from above. It is what it is. Starting tomorrow, he's your new partner. Show him the ropes."

Junior stuck out his hand. "I'm sure it'll be a pleasure working..."

He was cut off as Sam turned around, pushed him out of the way and headed out of the captain's door. She paused long enough at her desk to grab her jacket and then left the building.

Junior looked at Captain Erikson with a confused look on his face.

"Don't worry son. She'll warm up to you soon enough." Then he paused and thought about it for a moment. "If she doesn't shoot you first," he added.

4

FRIDAY

"I hate moving people out to this part of the County," Bryan said.

"Why?" Jose asked. "It's not a bad drive. There's a lot less traffic and look the beaches! Do you see those hot young things strutting around in those skimpy little bikinis?"

"Yeah, like you've got a chance with any one of them. The girls on those beaches are used to being with guys that make more in an hour than you make in a month."

"That's cold, grandpa. Like ice. Old age is making you crotchety."

"I ain't your grandpa, and I'm not that old. After seventeen years of moving people's shit all over this part of the state, I've learned what to expect when people move to this neighborhood. You mark my word, when we get to this place, it's going to be some rich ass-hole that thinks his shit don't stink. He's going be on us like stink on shit, telling us how we need to watch out for how we handle all of his precious shit. You'll see."

The two men continued up Highway 1 until they reached Ocean View Drive. When Bryan turned down the road, Jose caught his first sight of the big houses and said, "I wonder what something like that goes for."

"Do you see the size of that place? With that view? If they paid less than fifty million for it I'll eat this truck."

That got a laugh out of Jose. As the men continued down Ocean View Drive, they continued discussing what kind of person would live out here. "I'm telling you, this guy is going be a first class jerk."

"Want to put money on that? Say, fifty dollars?"

"If you think you can afford to lose that much, sure. I'll take your money."

When they got to their destination, Bryan pulled the truck off to the side of the road and parked. Jose, being familiar with this routine, jumped out of the cab and set up the cones around the truck. As they walked up the driveway, Bryan began pointing out the hazards to look for when Jose was backing the truck up the driveway.

When they got to the front of the house, Bryan said, "Aw, shit!"

Jose, looking perplexed asked, "What's wrong?"

"There's no car in the driveway. That means we're going have to wait for the prick to show up."

"Maybe not. He might have parked in the garage. Besides, look. The front door is open."

"Alright, I'll let him know we're here. You call dispatch and let them know we've made it to our destination and we'll start unloading ASAP. Then you can bring the truck up."

As Bryan got to the front door, he could hear Jose flirting with Cynthia, the receptionist. That kid better watch out. She is the boss' daughter, he thought. He rang the doorbell and called out, "Doctor Covington? We have your belongings."

After a few moments and no response, he pushed the door open a little bit further and called out, "Doctor Covington?" When there was still no response, he stepped inside. Sometimes these rich people will leave notes as to where to put things.

"Doctor Covington?" he called again. He walked farther into the living room, listening for some sound, some noise that would indicate that someone was there.

After a few seconds of straining his ears, he continued to the end of the room and turned the corner leading to the great room.

As he looked down at the floor, realization hit him and he let out a long scream at the sight of what lay before him.

5

"I can't believe they've got me training a kid," Sam said to her therapist with contempt. "And he's only been a cop for two years! Do you know how long it took me to become a detective?"

"Yes, Sam. I do," he commiserated. "It took you eight years. And do you know what I said when they made you my partner?"

"I'm afraid to ask."

"I said that I couldn't believe they were sticking me with some chick-y-poo from San Francisco. I knew you had to be some rich snob trying to prove yourself down here in L. A. I knew that you had to be trouble. Maybe you had authority issues; maybe you lacked discipline. But I knew that whatever the problem was that kept you in the uniform for eight years was now going to be my problem. But I was wrong. From the beginning, you were a better officer than I had expected. You had the right mind set and you're one of the best detectives I've ever seen. But you didn't stop there. You continued to push yourself, to become even better. And look how much you've grown in the last six years. You are by far the best detective LAPD has got. I would expect no less. I trained you, after all."

"Yeah, but only for the first two years… I mean… I…"

"Don't even go there! It was not your fault what happened that day. I didn't blame you then, and I don't blame you now. Besides, I have a career that I never would have dreamed of without your help. In a way, you taught me almost as much as I taught you," he said with a smile.

"Hey," Sam said with mock offence. "But seriously, I'm not sure I can deal with training a rookie detective. He's only twenty-two. And at least I had eight years on the force."

"You got me there," Darryl said with a smile. "Just give it some time. He might surprise you. You surprised me."

Sam's phone began to play, "If I shot you in the head, would it make you dead… If I shot you in the leg…"

"New ring tone?" Darryl asked.

"Yeah," she nodded. "It's Shot, by the Buckin' Fastards™."

Sam hit the answer button and said, "Franklin."

"Sam, this is Erikson. We've got a mess here, and I want you on point for this one. I'm texting you the address now. Be prepared, Sam. You're going to be dealing with something like you've never seen before. Hell, I've never seen anything like this."

"On my way, Captain. Hey, did anyone call Junior yet?"

"No, we left that treat for you," Erikson said and hung up the phone.

Sometimes, she really did hate that man. And what was

23

he doing at a crime scene? For the captain to come out himself, it could only mean one of two things. This was bound to be a high profile murder, or a particularly gruesome one. Then she paused and thought, or both.

Sam dialed up Junior's number. He answered it on the first ring.

"Detective Evans speaking," he said.

"Junior, its Sam" she said. "We've got one. I'm texting you the address. I'll be there in thirty minutes. I know this is your first one and you're all hot and bothered to get in there and pop your cherry on it, but don't go in until I get there."

"Why do you call me Junior?" he asked. "You know, I'm just as qualified as…"

"You are not as qualified as I am," Sam said with a snarl. "If you were, you would've have known just how little you know about police work. And I'll call you Junior until I see clear evidence that you know your ass from a hole in the ground. Now get moving. And don't go in until I get there!"

"What I meant is that I can handle any situation," Junior said with a cold levelness in his voice. "I am a detective after all."

"Then handle this. Get your ass up there," Sam said, and hung up the phone.

6

It took Sam forty minutes to get to the address the captain had given her. She drove past the moving truck and turned into the driveway, past the "for sale" sign posted by Brookhurst Realty, complete with its all too familiar picture of Michael Brookhurst. The signs were designed in such a way that when you drove up, from either direction, Michael was inviting you to turn down the driveway, complete with his outstretched arm. On top of the sign, was the word SOLD. No doubt about it now; this had to be a high profile murder. Brookhurst Realty wouldn't touch a property unless it had a value of at least fifty million. One hundred million if it was on the coast or with acreage. This place looked like it had both.

As she pulled up to the house, she could see several patrol cars, the coroner's van and Junior's Camaro all parked in the driveway. An officer was speaking with two men in uniforms that matched the logo on the side of the truck at the street.

As she walked up the path to the front door, she noticed that Junior was not outside waiting for her.

Of course! He had gone in. And he wondered why she called him Junior.

As the thought hit her mind, Junior came running out the front door, threw his face into a planter box, and lost his lunch.

"I told you to wait for me," she said as she walked passed him. With his head still buried in the planter box, Junior extended a middle finger in Sam's general direction.

"Captain, where are you hiding at?" Sam yelled as she walked into the house. Several officers were taking pictures of the scene, of scrapings on the walls and attempting to lift prints from various parts of the house. Captain Erikson stepped out from around the corner of what appeared to be either the living room, or the dining room, only much, much larger.

"Over here Sam" he said meeting her halfway to the front entryway. "The movers showed up this morning to deliver the furniture for one Blake Covington. Doctor Blake Covington. Other than that, we're not really sure about anything at this point. For all we know, Doctor Covington maybe our perp. He certainly would fit the bill. Jack got here just before you did. I filled him in on what we know so far. He's already started his investigation."

"Doesn't he need to get the body back to the lab to do that? And what do you mean the doctor fits the bill?"

"Not for most of it. And you'll see what I mean. Jack will fill you in on the rest. Hey Jack, come here."

Jack Adams, the Los Angeles County Coroner stepped out from behind the same wall that the captain had appeared from a moment ago.

"Glad to see that they have you leading up this investigation, Sam. This is one you're going to have to see to believe."

As he led Sam to the crime scene, he said, "The first guy said that when he walked up, the front door was open. He went in, and called out for Doctor Covington. When he rounded the corner, this is what he saw."

From the way the captain had talked, and from the re-action Junior had upon seeing the scene, Sam thought she had prepared herself for whatever might be around the corner. She had expected to see carnage everywhere. She expected blood to be all over the room; on the floor, on the walls, maybe even on the ceiling. She expected to see the evidence of what some deranged psychopath had managed to spread throughout the room. She had been on scenes like that before. They all had. Well, all of them except for Junior. And if he was going to react like that to a little blood maybe she wouldn't have to train him for much longer, she hoped. But the others were seasoned profes-sionals. They were acting like they had never been on a scene before. What could have gotten them so worked up?

At first glance, Sam didn't seem to realize what sat in front of her. What she saw was a collection of eight ma-son jars, sitting on the floor in a half circle in front of the fireplace. The jars were filled with a deep, red liquid. Just inside of the half circle of jars, were neat rows, lined up of different colors. There was one section that looked whitish, another one, reddish-black and a third of varying colors. The whitish ones were relatively thin, whereas the reddish-black ones tended to be thicker. The third appeared to be different shapes and sizes and they appeared to resemble organs. In front of that, was what looked like a neatly fold-ed empty leather duffel bag. Only when she got closer, did she realize that what lay before her, spread out on the ground, were the bones, muscles, organs, blood and skin of a dissected human being.

"Sam, take a look at this."

"What the hell is this?"

"I'll need to get these pieces back to the lab to be certain, but for now my best guess is that you're looking at is death by vivisection. But that's not the interesting part."

"That's not the interesting part?" She was almost in hysterics now.

"No, that part begins right here. Come take a look. Our killer left us a message."

As she approached where Jack was kneeling, he unfolded what looked like a leather duffel bag and held it up. It was human skin that had been tanned. She could see several words carved out of the skin. In what looked like stencil, it read, "**LOOK WHAT I CAN DO.**"

"Oh my God!" she said.

7

Sam tried to understand what it was that she was seeing. She was in a daze. A mental homicidal overload. When she pulled herself together, she shook her head, as if to clear it, and asked, "You said you thought this was death by what?"

"Vivisection. It's from the Latin word vivus meaning alive and sectio meaning cutting. Basically, your victim was surgically dismantled while he was still alive. Take a look at the grouping of muscles. These were removed from the bone with meticulous care. Not one of them is cut. They were scraped away at both the origin and insertion, then laid out in order. And do you see the black marks on the muscles? On all of them?"

"You mean where it looks as if they've been burned? Yeah?"

"Good eye. These tissues have been burned. Cauterized, to be more specific. In other words, this victim's blood was still flowing through his veins while his body was being taken apart."

"That sounds like it would be incredibly painful."

"Beyond imagination. I'd be surprised if the pain alone didn't kill him." Jack turned his attention away from the muscles and bones and began to sort through the organs.

"Whoa! Take a look at this!"

"What?"

"Right here, on the heart. Do you see these burn marks? One grouping here at the top and the other grouping here on the side?"

"More cauterizing?"

"No. See the round shapes? See how the burns are overlapping each other but only in these two spots?"

"Something tells me I'm not going to like what you say next."

"You're right. You're not. Your victim went into cardiac arrest, no doubt a physiological response to the pain he was suffering. These marks indicate that he was resuscitated, at least twice. But, Sam, this is the part that's going to keep me up at night," he said as he turned back towards the leathered skin and picked it up. "As you can see, this skin has been tanned. That's a process that takes a minimum of one to two weeks. These tissues were separated from their skin within the past 24-36 hours. My best guess at this point would be sometime between ten p.m. Wednesday and two a.m. Thursday."

"Wait a minute," she said with dawning realization. "Are you saying what I think you're saying? There's more than one victim here?"

"That's right."

"Geez. We've got one sick bastard on our hands here.

Clear evidence of torture? This sounds personal. Can you tell for sure who our victim was?"

"Not until I get these parts back to the lab. I need to check with Cedar-Sinai. They should have Dr. Covington's blood type. If his is the same blood type as our puzzle piece's, then I'll run a DNA test to see if we've got a match."

"And if it's not a match?"

"Then you'll need to start asking where the doctor is. Whoever did this had either advanced medical training, or a lot of time to practice."

"But if someone was practicing to kill like this, then where are the other bodies?"

"Exactly."

"But the doctor would have the skills to do this?"

"Yes, he would. Like I said before, I'll know a lot more once I get this mess back to the lab, but for now, there are a couple of things I know for sure. Number one, we've got at least two victims. Number two, the murder was not committed here."

"I picked up on that too. Let me know when you know for sure who he was. I'm going to grab some prints off of the leathered message board," Sam said as she turned towards the door. "Hey Junior, get your ass in here. You're not going to learn anything new by revisiting breakfast out there," she called out.

Junior walked in looking pale. She called him back over

to the scene. "Tell me what you see," she said.

Junior's eyes swept the room. A wave of nausea revisited him and he had to grab the wall for support. "There's parts all over," he said shakily.

Sam replied as if she were speaking to a three year old child. Or an adorable puppy. "Very good, Junior. What else do you see?"

"There are parts of a human body on the carpet of the large room," he said with a crackle in his voice, clearly trying to pull himself together. "There's a long scrape in the wood on the wall opposite the kitchen. Above the fireplace there's a champagne glass with lipstick on it." He turned around to face the kitchen. "There's a second champagne glass, probably the victim's, on the counter next to a champagne bottle, sitting next to a silver ice bucket. And on the cabinet door fronts there is another long scrape." He walked through the kitchen and down the hall. "There's a third scrape on the wall here."

"Not bad," she said. "But I have two questions for you. The first is, what about the stain in the big room on the carpet?"

What stain? is what he wanted to say. He quickly looked around, spotted the stain and said, "Maybe someone spilled something when they were showing the house."

"Do you even use that thing between your ears?" Sam said with heavy sarcasm. "Think for a second! If I had to take a guess, I'd say that this home sold for in excess of one hundred million dollars. Do you really think that they would let a stain be on the carpet while they were showing the house? That stain happened after it sold. I'd bet money that is where one of those glasses fell on the floor. There was probably some kind of drug in it." Sam looked at the tech collecting prints, pointed to the carpet and said, "Make sure you get a sample of that stain." She refocused her attention on Junior. "Okay, second question: which room do you think the murder took place in?"

"The body's in the large room with the fireplace. That's where the stain is."

"So you think our victim was killed there?"

"Wasn't he?"

"Did you see any blood on the walls? Or on the carpet?"

"No."

"You've got to follow the evidence," Sam said, emphasizing every syllable while hitting the back of her right hand into the palm of her left. "Other than a stain on the floor and all of the parts of the body being in the large room, there's nothing here to indicate that he was killed in that room, or, from what I've seen, anywhere in this house."

"So where was he killed?"

"Our victims," she said, heavy on the s, "were killed elsewhere. Our priority now is identifying who it is that's out there," she said, pointing to the great room, "and who it is that put them there."

"How are we supposed to do that?"

"Jack is going to compare blood types of our jigsaw puzzle in there with the home owner's. If the blood types are a match, then he'll run the DNA to see if it's him. I'm going to talk to the movers. The arriving officer already pulled fingerprints from both glasses as well as the ice bucket. You pull the prints off the message board." Sam smiled inwardly as she watched Junior shudder. "We need to establish the identities of the victims. Jack will get that to us as soon as he can. We need to figure out where our victims were prior to this morning. When you're done, get the prints that the officers have collected and meet me back at the station. Run the prints while you wait for me, and have a name ready for me when I get there."

Junior headed in the direction of the pieces. Sam stepped outside and spoke with the driver of the moving truck. He told her the same thing he had told the other officer he had spoken with earlier; that they had arrived earlier in the day and that no one was here. There was no car in the driveway. When he got to the front of the house, the door was already open. He called out and no one responded. He went in and found the body. At that point he started to turn a little green. Sam thanked him for his time, and turned to leave.

As she got in her car and headed down the driveway, the questions began coming to her mind as they always do at the beginning of a new case. Was that Dr. Covington in there? Or, did he do that bit of handy work? If that is him lying in pieces on the floor, what did he do to piss someone off that bad? And what was with the second victim? Or, would that be the first victim? Whose red lipstick was on the glass?

Then the worst thought of all hit her.

Look what I can do.

That was the message the killer had left for them to find.

Look what I can do.

The killer was showing off his skills.

Look what I can do.

That's a taunt.

Look what I can do.

"Oh crap," Sam said with a reluctant, but accepting sigh. "Whoever did that isn't done yet," she said aloud and grabbed her cell phone.

8

As she pulled away from the house, Sam called Michael Brookhurst. He said that the sale of the property had gone off without a hitch. The doctor had offered to pay the full price for the home in cash, with a seven day close of escrow. The escrow officer they had used was his daughter Suzie. She was the manager of Capital Escrow on Sepulveda Boulevard in Culver City. They closed escrow on the property late Wednesday afternoon.

Sam made a quick mental note. From what Jack had said about the time the tissues were separated from their skin, Suzie had been with Blake only a few hours before his demise.

So there it was. His demise. She already knew that when the results came back, Jack would tell her that it had been Dr. Blake Covington laying in bits and pieces. And Suzie had been with him just before his demise. She may have been the last one to see him alive. She thanked Michael for his time, exchanged pleasantries and hung up.

As she drove down the hill towards Capitol Escrow, she turned on the radio. Ever since her days at U.C. Berkeley, she had been hooked on talk radio.

As an assignment for one of her psychology classes, she had been asked to listen to a talk radio program, and then write a paper about what she thought motivated the listening audience to call in and express their views. She had looked forward to the assignment with all the enthusiasm of someone preparing for a root canal. The night before the assignment was due, she finally summoned the energy to begin the assignment.

She had turned on KOSF, San Francisco's knock out talk radio station. Apparently, the host had had an argument with a caller a few weeks before. The caller had ranted and raved about how easy the job of talk radio host would be. The host had responded with a challenge: if the caller thought it was so easy to talk to people on air while having an intelligent conversation about a difficult topic, then they would arrange for him to sit in the host's seat and give it a try. Of all the nights she would pick to tune in, she chose to listen in on the night the challenge was to be met.

As it turned out, the young man had been very good. Although he could have picked any number of topics, he chose to open his broadcast with the words, "Can you imagine what a world without religion would look like?"

It had been a polarizing topic. Many people called in with such comments as, "Sacrilege" and "Blasphemy" while others expressed support for an idea whose time had come. He handled the callers like a seasoned professional. The discussion had been lively and entertaining. Before the hour was over, Sam was hooked on talk radio.

As luck would have it, Bill McKinley, the station manager for KKLA, "LA's hot talk at 1010 on the am dial," was on a business trip to the Bay Area that week. He had been listening to the show on his way to the airport, and had been so impressed with the young man, that he turned his rental car around and made the trip back into the city. He drove to the station and arranged to meet with the young man following the broadcast. By the time Sam had finished her paper, Los Angeles had a new voice in talk radio: Thomas Collins.

She made the drive to Culver City and pulled into Capital Escrow's parking garage. She was just about to enter the office when she received a call from Junior.

"Sam," he began.

"That's Detective Franklin," she snapped.

"Fine," he said. "Detective Franklin. I just got off the phone with Cedar-Sinai. Blake Covington's blood type was B negative. According to Dr. Adams, we have a preliminary match to the victim's blood in the jars. He said that when he gets the body back to the lab he'll begin DNA testing. They also said that Doctor Covington didn't show up for work yesterday or today."

"Interesting," Sam mused. "Did you get an ID off of the leathered skin?"

"I haven't even left the scene yet."

"So? You have a smart phone, don't you? Use the police database app. And get back to me as soon as you find out who that is," she said and then hung up the phone.

She entered Capital Escrow's office, and was greeted by Margie Rice, the office secretary.

Sam identified herself and asked to speak with Suzie Brookhurst. Margie invited Sam to take a seat while she called Ms. Brookhurst up front. After a few minutes a short blonde with a medium build came out. If this is Suzie, Sam thought to herself, there's no way she could have done that to the victim. At least she couldn't do that alone. That was quickly followed by the voice that always spoke to her. Darryl's voice. "Follow where the evidence takes you," it said.

"Hi, Detective Franklin? I'm Suzie Brookhurst. How can I help you?"

"Ms. Brookhurst, is there some place we can speak in private?"

"That depends, what is this regarding?"

"Do you know Blake Covington?"

"Yes, we closed on his property two days ago. Is there something wrong?"

"Why would you think that there would be anything wrong?"

"Look detective, I'm not stupid. Detectives don't make it a habit of asking me about my clients unless there's something wrong."

"This is true. Were there any problems with him?"

"Yeah, he was a first class, grade A asshole. I hated that man. I wish somebody would kill him. The world would be a better place if he were dead."

"Well congratulations. It looks like you got your wish."

"What? Blake's dead?" she asked, her eyes widening.

"Can we speak in private? Now?"

Suzie led her to her office where the two sat down. According to Suzie, Blake had been a real "pain in the ass" client. He had been demanding and condescending. He had treated everyone, including his own real estate agent, as if they were all beneath him. Nothing she could do for him was good enough. Even though they closed the property two days earlier than contractually required, he complained that she had taken too long. The day they closed escrow on the property, he signed the paperwork, took possession of the keys and then drove off as if he were a race car driver, nearly hitting a man walking his dog across the street in the process. Although she said she was sorry to hear that he had died, it was obvious that she wouldn't be shedding any tears over his death.

Sam asked her where she was Wednesday evening between eight p.m. and two a.m. Suzie said she went to a club with one of her friends to celebrate the house closing. She said she was there until about two. After that, she had gone home. Sam thanked her for her time, and said that if she had any other questions for Suzie, she would be in touch. Suzie made to get up from her desk, and Sam said not to bother. She said she would be fine walking herself out. As she turned to leave the office, Suzie reached for the phone. When Sam turned back to ask her who Blake's real estate agent had been, Suzie's eyes grew wide, like a child who is caught stealing the cookie they've been told they can't have. She decided to wait on asking anymore questions. For now.

As she headed for the front door, Margie, the secretary,

called out, "Detective Franklin? Can I speak with you a moment?"

Sam turned around and went to the desk. "Margie, right?" Sam asked. Margie nodded. "How can I help you?"

"Did I hear that correctly? Did you say that Doctor Covington was dead? Was he murdered?"

"Yes, it looks like it. We won't know for sure until some tests come back, but it does appear to be the case. Do you know anything about it? Maybe why anyone would want to kill him?"

"Well, he was a mean person. I didn't like him. It's just that," she hesitated, giving a nervous glance from side to side around the room. "It's just that when he left, I was in the supply closet, next to Ms. Brookhurst's office. I was getting supplies to restock the office for the next day. She didn't know I was in there."

"And you heard something."

Margie nodded, her eyes the size of saucers.

"What was it, Margie?"

"She had called Jane Woodman. You know, Doctor Covington's real estate agent? They're friends, you know."

"No, I didn't know who his real estate agent had been. You say that this Jane Woodman and Ms. Brookhurst are friends?"

Margie nodded. "Anyway, she tends to put her calls on

41

speakerphone, and they were complaining about how horrible he had been. Ms. Woodman had said it was time they taught him a lesson. But not just him. She said that they would teach all of the people like him a lesson."

"Did she they say what they had planned to do?"

"No. Ms. Brookhurst asked Ms. Woodman if she had anything in mind. She said she did, but that she didn't want to talk about it over the phone. She said that they would go over the details when they met in person at that Steampunk club they go hang out at."

"Do you know which club that is?"

"I think it's called The Underground Carriage™. It opened up about six months ago. Ms. Brookhurst and Ms. Woodman are always talking about going there, you know, after work, on weekends."

Sam thanked her for her time and the information and headed out to her car. So, Suzie wasn't being completely honest, she thought. What was she hiding? Could it have been her lipstick on the champagne glass above the mantel? Or was it, oh, what was her name? Jane; that was it. If what Margie had said was correct, it sounded like they would have an axe to grind with Blake. But was it enough to stir that kind of calculated rage? And did either of them have any kind of medical background? She made a mental note to have Junior do some background checking on Suzie and Jane to see if either of them had any medical training or if they had ties to anyone with such. She got in her car and ran an address search for the Underground Carriage™. When the address came up she punched it in to her GPS. She started up her car, pulled out of the parking lot and headed for the club. Even though it was close to noon and they probably weren't open yet, there had to be someone there to prep for this weekend's business.

9

When Sam arrived at the club, she was surprised to see so many cars in the parking lot. A Steampunk club not only open, but also busy at noon?

She went inside to find that the manager was holding a staff meeting. Lucky for her, it looked as if the entire staff was there. She excused the interruption, identified herself and asked to speak with the manager. He was a man about her age, dressed in all bronze with gears strategically placed on his costume. His eyes were painted with a brown eyeliner, and he had drawn in what appeared to be a zipper that went from the left nostril around and above both eyes before connecting with the right one. She asked if she could speak with whoever was working the club Wednesday night. He checked his tablet and called two people over.

Michelangelo, the bartender and Sabrina, the cocktail waitress had been working that night. They both remembered seeing Suzie and Jane. They were regulars at the club. Everybody knew those two.

"The strange thing was," Sabrina had said, "that they're usually out on the floor dancing, flirting with guys, stuff like that. Wednesday though, they were huddled up in the booth over there and were deep in conversation. When I brought them their drinks once, I caught some of what they were talking about. It sounded like they wanted to kill someone. At one point they had gotten into an argument. Jane got up and left around ten. Suzie finished her drink and then left about fifteen minutes after that."

So, Suzie told another lie, Sam thought. What else is Suzie trying to hide? Sam thanked the two for their time and she left the club. She was thinking about heading back over to the escrow office and confronting Suzie on her lies when her phone started ringing. A quick look down at her phone told her it was Junior. "What have you got for me?" she asked.

"The prints are back," Junior said. "You're not going to believe this."

"Why? What's wrong with the prints?"

"I don't know what to make of this Sam."

"I don't know what to make of this, Detective . You haven't earned the right to call me Sam. And what do you mean you don't know what to make of this?"

"Well, *Detective*," Junior said, clearly annoyed, "It's just that our victim, the skin, I mean. His fingerprints came back and they say that he's one John Porter. He was a property manager in Palo Alto. You know, the San Francisco Bay Area?"

"Yes Junior, I know where Palo Alto is."

"Well a missing person's report was filed on him two months ago."

"That is strange. What's the tanned skin of a property

manager from the Bay Area doing at our crime scene down here? And where has he been for the last two months?"

"I don't know, but that's not all. The print from the glasses came back."

"Oh wait. Let me guess. The prints on the glasses belong to someone who died in the eighteen hundreds?"

"No. The prints on the glass that was on the counter belong to Blake Covington. Only they were kind of smudged like someone with gloves picked up the glass after him."

"Interesting. What about the glass with the lipstick on it? The one above the fireplace?"

"She's still alive. The prints on that glass belong to a Margret Hudson. Sister Margret Hudson. She lives in a convent in Modesto."

"Are you trying to tell me that that mess we left this morning was the act of a nun? What the hell is going on here?"

"No, I've already checked on her. She's been up in Modesto during the time both victims were unaccounted for."

"Okay," Sam said breathing a heavy sigh. "We need to talk to her. I hope you don't have plans for this weekend. It looks like we're going to be making a trip up north. We'll leave tomorrow, and we can take my car."

"But I've got tickets to…"

"And, in the meantime," Sam interrupted before he could continue, "I need you to run a check on a couple of people for me. See if Suzie Brookhurst or Jane Woodman or any of their known associates have any kind of medical training. Let me know as soon as you find something."

"Fine," Junior said, completely disgruntled.

Sam hung and up leaned the car's seat back as far as she could. She started to rub her temples. None of this makes sense, she thought. What's the connection? Why would a nun's fingerprints be on a glass at a homicide scene near Malibu, with at least two dead bodies, or parts thereof, one from Palo Alto and the other presumably from Los Angeles? And what role did Suzie and Jane play in this, if any at all?

She sat up quickly as a sudden thought struck her. Did Blake have any family members? Now that Blake was dead, assuming that was him in little pieces all over the floor, what would happen to all of his money? Did he make out a will? Would any surviving family members get it? She called Junior back.

"Detective Evans speaking."

"Junior, its Sam."

"Hold your horses. It's going to take me longer than five seconds to do everything you asked me to do."

"No shit, Sherlock. Shut up and listen, and you just might find out why I called you. Did Blake have any family members?"

"I was just checking into that. The reports I'm seeing show that he had a brother. David Covington. Apparently they were never close, but it got much worse after last year."

"Why? What happened last year?"

"It looks like their father died in a traffic accident."

"Couldn't they make peace with each other at a time like that?"

"A year ago is when he died. But it was the events after his death that made things much worse between them. When his daddy died…" he started to say with disdain in his voice.

Sam cut him short with an angry tone he hadn't yet heard before. "You mean when their *father* died," she snapped.

Junior hesitated. "Um, yes. When their father died," he said cautiously, "he had a huge estate. By some estimates over two billion dollars. Blake got the lion's share. David received just five million dollars. Blake got everything else. There were no other relatives or heirs."

"Geez. Only getting five million of a two billion dollar estate? If that's not motive for the brother then I don't know what is. Do we know if Blake had a will?"

"Not anything that I can find."

"I wonder, what happens to the estate if Blake's no longer in the picture and he doesn't have a will?"

"Under California law it would go through the court system for a given period of time," Junior started to explain. "Then, if no one makes a claim on the estate, the money would go to the descendants of the decedent, or if there were no descendants, it would pass to the next of kin, in this case, his brother," he said with a legal expertise that was beyond his years.

Trying to hide her astonishment at his knowledge of inheritance law, she said, "That gives David motive."

"Do you want me to go talk to him?"

"No I'll go talk to David. Find out who Blake Covington's lawyer was. I want to talk to him, too. I want to see if Blake made a will. And if he did, I want to know who the beneficiaries are."

"Okay, but detective, can I ask you a question? You're assuming that the pieces we found this morning are that of Dr. Covington. I know that the blood types are a match, but I heard Dr. Adams say that whoever did this had to have surgical skills. Why aren't you looking at the doctor as a possible suspect, instead of as the victim?"

"That's the first time I've heard you ask a question that sounded like it came from a detective. Let me ask you this: even if you had enough money to buy that place for cash, would you stage a crime, that hideous, in your house, within hours after you bought it? Would you shout out to the world, 'I'm Blake Covington. I just bought this place. Look what I can do?'"

"No. I wouldn't."

"That's why I think he's the one in pieces. But you do bring up a good point. After you're done getting me the name of the lawyer, check in at Cedar-Sinai. See if any of his co-workers, fellow doctors, nurses, or even support staff had an issue with him."

"Okay, run background check and see if Ms. Brookhurst or Ms. Woodman or any of their known associates have any kind of medical training, check on who the lawyer is and talk to the hospital staff. Sounds like an easy day, Sam."

"That's detective. Got it?" she said with a snarl in her voice. "Just because I said you had a good idea doesn't make us equals. And no it's not an easy day. But you're a detective. Go detect."

"Fine. *Detective* . I just don't understand, when are you going to…" Click. Sam hung up the phone. She started up the car and drove out of the parking lot in the direction of Covington Oil. It was time to pay a visit to David Covington.

10

"Detective Evans, where is your Partner?" Captain Erikson asked, as he approached Junior's desk, flanked by two women.

"She's on her way to talk to David Covington, the brother of the…"

"She's supposed to be training you. You're not going to learn to be the right kind of detective on your own. I just got word from the mayor. This case is our number one priority. I'm assigning Detectives Daniels and Sheppard here to assist with this case."

Detective Daniels stepped forward and reached out her hand. "Jennifer Daniels. Pleased to meet you. This is my partner Nina Sheppard."

"Richard Evans. Likewise," he said, shaking both of their hands.

"What has she got you working on?" Erikson asked.

"I'm supposed to be finding out if either Suzie Brookhurst or Jane Woodman have any kind of medical training. Then I've got to find out who Blake Covington's attorney is, and then I'm supposed to go to Cedar-Sinai Medical Center and find out if anyone had anything against Dr. Covington."

51

"Who are Suzie Brookhurst and Jane Woodman?"

"They were his escrow and real estate agents, respectively."

"That's too much for you to do on your own on your first day as a detective," Erikson said. "Sheppard, I want you to look into Suzie Brookhurst and Jane Woodman's background, and then find out who Blake Covington's attorney was. Daniels, take Evans to Cedar-Sinai and ask around. I'll talk to Sam when she gets back to the station."

The captain turned and walked back to his office. Detective Daniels looked at Junior and said, "You are so dead when Sam hears about this."

11

Sam pulled into the Covington Oil parking lot around three o'clock, Friday afternoon. She had to park away from the building. A large crane was situated up near the front of the building. It had removed the Covington Oil sign and was replacing it with one that read, "The Okane Corporation". A man that looked like he was in his mid to late forties was looking up at the sign, shaking his head in disbelief. She walked up to him.

"New sign?" she asked him.

"Yes. Along with everything else that's new," he said bitterly.

"What do you mean?"

"I mean a year ago, I was on top of the world. I thought I was being groomed to take over this company. I thought my father could see how hard I worked to make this company what it was."

"And then what happened?"

"I'm sorry, but I don't make a habit of telling my personal business to a complete stranger. Who are you?"

"Samantha Franklin," she said, holding up her detective's shield. "Detective Samantha Franklin. Los Angeles

Police Department, Homicide Division. And you are?"

"David Covington."

"So, David, may I call you David? What happened?"

"Homicide division? What you think someone intentionally killed my father last year?"

"No, I'm not here to investigate his death. I just have a few questions for you. Like what happened after your father died?"

"I got to see what my father really thought of me. He died suddenly, and in his will, he gave just about everything to my brother. He set his will up in such a way that if I contested any part of it, I got nothing. Then my brother went and sold off the company. Today, the new owners gave me this."

He held at arm's length a pink slip. "Notice of termination" it read at the top. "As I'm leaving, I see this crane pull up with that new sign. I think if my brother showed his ugly face right now," he stammered and hesitated and then said, "Well, I'm not sure what I'd do to him."

"It sounds like your brother is a real jerk. It sounds like you really hate him."

"Hate doesn't even begin to describe what I feel towards him. I hope he dies a slow, painful death. And I hope I can be there to watch when it happens."

"So, were you?"

"Excuse me?"

"Were you there David? Did you watch? Or maybe I should ask, where were you between ten pm Wednesday night and two am Thursday?"

"What are you saying? Did something happen to Blake? Is he dead?"

"We believe that Blake was murdered," she said, nodding her head. "We'll know more after the DNA results come back."

"DNA results? Don't you know if it's him? Do you need me to come and identify the body?"

"Mr. Covington, I'm not going to discuss the details of an ongoing investigation, particularly with someone who may be a person of interest. Until we can establish where you were on Wednesday night, please just answer the question. If you prefer I could take you own to the station and we could discuss it there."

"Am I under arrest?"

"No, David. You're not. I just have a few questions for you."

"Then I'll direct you to ask any questions you may have to my attorney, Will Dixon. I'm done here," he said. Then he turned and got into his car and drove away.

12

As David began to drive away, Sam's phone rang. "Franklin here," she said.

"Sam, what the hell do you think you're playing at?" came the voice from the other end of the phone.

"Good to hear from you too, Captain. So what did Junior say when he came crying to you?"

"Do you know I found him on his first day investigating alone? You're supposed to be showing him how we do things, not sending him out by himself. Is that how Darryl taught you?"

"Low blow, Captain! Keep Darryl out of this. I didn't ask for you to throw Junior into my lap."

"First off, don't ever talk to me like that again or I'll bust you so low you'll be wishing you were a beat cop. Second, you were assigned to work with Detective Evans. Work with means work together. Get your ass back here and teach him the way Darryl taught you," he said.

"I'll be there as soon as I talk to David Covington's attorney. His office is on the way back to the station," she lied. She had no idea where his office was.

"Fine. But when you're done get your ass back here," he

said and slammed down the phone.

That whining, little son of a bitch, she thought. He went crying to the captain. I'm going to wring his little neck. But I'll deal with him later. I've got bigger fish to fry.

She ran a search for Will Dixon, esquire. After a few seconds, the search engine came back with his address. She hit the get directions button on her cell phone. Twenty minutes later she pulled into the parking lot of Dixon Law.

A well-dressed man carrying a briefcase stepped out of the office as she approached. As he turned to lock the door, she approached him and asked, "Excuse me. Are you Will Dixon?"

"Attorney at law. You must be Detective Samantha Franklin. David called me a few minutes ago. He said you would be stopping by."

"Do you have a minute for a few questions Mr. Dixon?"

"If they're quick. It's Friday and I'm looking forward to my weekend."

"I was wondering if you could give me some insight into the relationship between David Covington and his brother Blake."

"They weren't fond of each other."

"Could you elaborate on that?"

"Simply put, Detective, they did not like each other. I warned him not to do that, but he was pig headed and stubborn."

"Excuse me?"

"I'm referencing, of course, the last will and testament that Richard made. Look detective, it was no secret that the boys didn't get along. Richard made things worse by plainly showing his favoritism toward Blake. When he made the will, he gave David five million dollars. The rest went to Blake. I told him that it was a bad idea. But like always, Richard did what he wanted to do."

"And then he died suddenly?"

"Yes. There was a nasty traffic accident. A big rig blew a tire, flipped over and landed on his car. He died instantly."

"And how did David and Blake react when they found out what was in their father's will?"

"David just about lost it. He was screaming and yelling. He threatened Blake. But then he calmed down quickly, once he found out about the poison pill."

"The what?"

"Poison pill. It's a term we in the legal field use. It basically means that if David tried to contest the will, he would have received nothing. When Blake found out he had sole ownership of the rest of the assets, including the oil and transportation companies, he spoke with me about liquidating all of his assets. We closed a deal with the Okane Corporation out of Japan last month. Blake netted just over one point nine billion dollars."

"Wow. And how did David take the news?"

"Well, you must understand Detective. At first David wanted to buy the company from Blake. But what he was offering was nowhere near what The Okane Corporation brought to the table. In the end, Blake took the higher offer. David was angry to say the least."

"Angry enough to kill?"

"I doubt it. While it's true that David has a temper, he's always in control of it. He's not the type to go off halfcocked and shoot anybody, if that's what you're asking."

"I didn't say anybody had been shot. Did Blake have a will?"

"Not to my knowledge, although I had suggested repeatedly to him that he should do so."

"Alright. Thank you for your time. I'll be in touch if I have any more questions for you," she said and walked back to the car.

Sam got into her car and headed back to the station. She needed to start mapping things out on the murder board. Her mind was racing with thoughts of the case.

To take apart another human being like that took meticulous effort, both in planning and in execution. The individual in question would have to have some intense rage, but also an incredible amount of self-control. Could someone with that much rage, that much anger be in that much control of him or herself?

Clearly, David had motive. He certainly would have had

that kind of intense rage. And according to Will Dixon, he had the ability to remain in control of himself. To do that to his brother, after everything else, was possible, but what rage would he have towards a property manager in Palo Alto?

Then again, Sabrina had said that Jane Woodman and Suzie Brookhurst had been talking about killing someone. And Suzie did lie to me. I'm going to need to talk to Jane.

And what was the connection between a doctor from Los Angeles and a property manager from Palo Alto that went missing two months ago? And how did a nun from Modesto fit in to this? Somehow Sam couldn't imagine a nun doing that to two people. And the glass. Was the glass planted? As if to throw us off? Or was it tied to one of the murders? If it's from a nun, how did the perpetrator get a hold of it? Was there a third victim? A victim that is somehow related to the other two victims? No, that doesn't make any sense. The nun is still alive.

It seemed like nobody liked this guy. The general feeling is that everybody wanted Blake dead. I wonder if anyone at his work hated him enough to do this to him, she thought.

She picked up the phone and dialed Junior's number. When he answered, she jumped in before he could speak. "Junior, what'd you find out at the hospital?"

"Well *detective*," he said, sounding as if he was still sulking from the recent tongue lashing and being left alone. "It seems that he had very few people who were surprised to find out he was dead. Most of the people I spoke with thought he was a first class ass wipe. The others thought even less of him than that."

"Anyone in particular that might have a grudge against him?"

"There was one. It seems that a Doctor Justin Wilde had been trying to get the position of chief surgeon when the spot opened up a couple of weeks ago."

"I know him," Sam interrupted. "He's the doctor that took the bullet out of…"

After a moment of silence Junior said, "Detective? Are you there?"

She seemed to gather herself. "Yes I'm here. You were saying something about Dr. Wilde?"

"Yes. He was trying to become the chief surgeon, but he lost the position to Dr. Covington. He seemed to be really upset about it at the time. I spoke with him and asked him about his whereabouts. He said he was with his girl-friend at the Hyatt near LAX. I checked with the hotel and they confirmed that the two of them arrived at the hotel at eight Wednesday night. They ordered room service a half an hour later. They stayed in the room until they checked out at six the next morning."

"Did you check the security cameras? Maybe he snuck out?"

"Detective Sheppard is working on that."

"How did you convince her to do that?"

"I didn't. The captain came down here himself and put her and Daniels on the case to assist us with the investigation."

He must really want this case wrapped up quick, she thought. "Yeah, I heard you talked to him."

"Hey, he found me working the case from my desk, Detective. I didn't go crying to him, if that's what you're insinuating."

"Okay, is there anything else that I should know about? Like where are we on finding out, did Ms. Brookhurst or Ms. Woodman had any kind of medical training?"

"Yes. Jane Woodman went to Cerritos College for their nursing program. She graduated in 2003, top of her class, but then she never went on to become a nurse. It looks like she didn't even bother to take her NCLEX."

"Her what?"

"Her NCLEX. It the test that she would have had to take to become a nurse."

"Jack said that whoever did this would have to have extensive training. Does she have any other training?"

"Medically, no. However, in 2004 Ms. Brookhurst took a hazardous materials training class."

"Interesting. I wonder why she did that. Do either of them have any other connection to the medical field? Friends? Family? Boyfriend? Girlfriend?"

"No. Jane was an only child. Both parents deceased. Hit and run driver in 2003."

"That doesn't seem to fit the description of who we're looking for. Okay, I'll be at the station in twenty minutes. I want to go over this again tonight and then we can make plans to head north tomorrow morning."

"Detective, its Friday night. We've been working this case since about eight thirty this morning. It's almost six now."

"Suck it up, buttercup. You're a detective now. Tomorrow we head north. We've got a nun to interview in Modesto and then we'll head to Palo Alto to talk to a property management company. If we're lucky we can be done in a couple of days. But tonight we need to review what we're looking at and outline our trip. We should be done before ten." As she hung up the phone, she could hear Junior let out a tirade of expletives.

Sam pulled onto the 10 eastbound and got off at the Figueroa exit downtown. She pulled into the parking garage shared by the LAPD and the crime lab. She went inside and saw Jack still in his lab coat working franticly.

"Jack, I'm surprised to see you. I thought you would be out of here by now," Sam said as she entered the lab.

"Normally I would be. But I got the directive from the chief himself an hour ago. He came down here personally and said that he wants everything else put on hold until we get the results from this DNA test. He said we have to know for sure whether we're looking at Dr. Covington as a victim or as a suspect. He's even ordered us to run the

DNA without batching. 'Set everything else aside,' he said. 'This is priority number one,'" Jack said imitating the chief, shaking his hand in the air. "We should have the results for you by Sunday morning at the latest."

"Thanks Jack. Let me know when they're in," she said. "Have you had a chance to go over the remains yet?"

"Actually, I have. And I've found some interesting things. Come over here and let me show you what I've got so far."

She followed him through the double doors into the main lab where there were four sets of tables on the left side of the room and four sets of tables on the right side. On the back wall were the individual refrigerators where the bodies were kept prior to examination. He led her over to the two tables in the back left corner of the room. On the table on the left was the former property manager, now leathered message board. Jack brought Sam over to the table on the right. The pieces from this morning had been somewhat reassembled to approximately where they normally would have been on a person.

"As we knew before, the skin from our pieces is missing. From the message left for us I would venture to say that it is currently undergoing the tanning process. Do you notice what's missing?"

Sam took a moment to examine the parts laid out before her. She hadn't taken an anatomy class; Jack knew this. It must be something rather obvious. She quickly scanned the feet, legs and mid-section. Everything seemed to be there. She looked at the chest. It looked as normal as you could expect for a dissected chest. She got to the head and saw what Jack had wanted her to see. The skull had been cut open. "Where's the brain," she asked?

"It wasn't returned to the scene. If I had to make an educated guess I'd say whoever did this has it, along with the skin."

"Like a trophy?"

"No. The brain can be used in the tanning process. We found traces of vecuronium and succinylcholine in the blood. Combined they would have acted to paralyze the victim while keeping him alive and conscious through the whole ordeal. When we found those drugs, we compared it to our leathered skin. It also had traces of those drugs on it. If the manner of death for him was in the same fashion as it was for our pieces, there would not have been enough time for the drugs to show up in the skin unless the skin had been tanned with the brain of the first victim."

"That sounds disgusting. Is that it?"

"No. We also found traces of clonazepam in the blood. When we found it, I checked the carpet. The stain on it was from a champagne that had high doses of clonazepam in it. If the victim had been drinking it in any substantial quantity, say a glass or two, it would have only been a matter of minutes before he became incapacitated."

"Alright, thanks for the update. Let me know if you find anything else," she said and she headed for the door.

"I will," Jack said, returning to his bits on the table.

When she got back to the station, Sam grabbed some

food from the taco truck sitting outside. She took it up to her desk, and handed Junior a burrito and a cola. Of course, Junior was pouting about having to work through a Friday night, but he had to learn. That was the life of a detective.

By the time they had called it a night, a bit past nine, they had mapped out all they knew about the two victims and the list of suspects. The list of known suspects. The thought that kept bothering her was, how is it that any of these suspects had ties to three very different people in three very different areas of California? Maybe tomorrow it would make more sense.

13

SATURDAY

Sam pulled up to Junior's apartment at a quarter past four, Saturday morning. He was standing in front of his apartment building looking like the proverbial tourist in New York City, about to get mugged. "And he thinks he's just as much a detective as I am," she muttered, shaking her head. To Sam, the difference was clear.

She was dressed in a khaki, button downed shirt and a pair of black slacks. She had a small gym bag that she was using for her personal items and a change of clothes.

Junior was dressed from the top down in a floral Hawaiian shirt, white clam digger pants and flip flops. He was carrying a large grey gym bag and a large pull behind suitcase on wheels.

He tried to open the door to the back seat of her car, but it was locked. He opened the front door, ducked his head inside, intending to ask her to unlock the door, but before he could speak, she said, "Look Junior. We're not going on vacation. You're not a tourist. Get your ass back in there and change into something that makes you look like a professional. And loose the extra luggage. We're not going to be there for a week."

He opened his mouth to protest but she held up her right hand in the stop motion, pointed her finger back towards his apartment and then waved good-bye. He stood up and slammed the car door as he turned away. She rolled down the window and yelled, "Don't slam my car door!" He ignored her and headed back inside to change.

Fifteen minutes later he came out dressed in a navy blue polo shirt, black trousers and black shoes. He had a smaller version of the gym bag he had brought out earlier, only with no additional luggage. "Is this better?" he asked with heavy attitude as he opened the door. He was pouting again.

Sam let out a deep sigh. God, she hated raising twenty year old children. "Junior, before we go anywhere, we need to talk. I know you are twenty years old…"

"I'm twenty-two," he snapped at her.

"Okay, I know that you are twenty-two ," she corrected. "And I know that you are a detective." God only knows how you managed to pull off that bit of magic, she thought. "I also know that I'm not your favorite person in the world, and to be quite honest, you're not mine, either. I didn't ask to have you assigned to me, and you have shown me very little that suggests that you are anywhere near qualified to be my partner. It bugs me to no end that you made detective after two years of being on the force. But, you were assigned to me. I was informed that I get to train you. Whoopee for me."

She paused to let that sink in. When she could see the information register on his face, she continued, "But as a friend of mine reminded me yesterday, I too was a rookie detective once. I didn't always think the way a detective should think. Yes, we both qualified as detectives. But that's just the beginning.

"You need to adjust your whole mindset. I had to do the same when I was a rookie detective too. I will try to be more patient with you. But for God's sake, you need to use your brain. You want respect. You feel that you're a detective, and that you've earned it. And that's all well and good when you're dealing with the uniformed officers and the general public. And if anyone from either of those two groups doesn't respect you, I'll be the first one getting in their face about it.

"But it doesn't work that way with the rest of the detectives. You haven't proven yourself to me or to any one of them. Now, instead of wearing your heart on your sleeve and getting your feelings hurt every time I get on your case about something, why don't you try to learn from the experience? The respect you want, the respect you feel you've earned, it will come, eventually. But not if you stick out your lower lip and pout like a baby who didn't get his way. Now get in the car. I wanted to be on the road half an hour ago."

He put his lone gym bag into the back seat and then got in the car. For the next fifteen minutes he said nothing. He just kept looking out the window. Finally he said in a low, quiet voice, "I'm trying. You have no idea how hard this is. You have no idea what I've been through to get here."

She wanted to slap the stupid right out of him. Instead she took a second to calm down and said, "You're right. It's true, I have no idea what you have been through, nor do I know what you are going through now. Just as you have no idea what I've gone through, nor do you have any idea of what I'm going through now. I'm not you. You're not me.

Even if what each of us have been through is similar, each person handles things differently. So no, I couldn't know what you're going through.

"We've all gone through our own personal hell to get to where we are today. We all have things that torture our souls. They're the things that keep us up at night. They're the thing we would do different if we could, but because we can't, we ignore them. We bury them deep inside, where they continue to torture us. You either learn to live with it and move on, or you let it consume you to the point where you can't even move. It's a fact of life that we all eventually have to face. But while you're in this car, working with me on this or any other case, I need to know that you'll have my back like I'll have yours. Got it?"

"Fine," he said. "Do you mind if I try and get a little more sleep?"

"Help yourself, if you can," she said as she turned on the radio to her normal station, hoping she hadn't missed the news at the top of the hour. She had.

They were crossing over the Ventura freeway headed north on I-5 when the familiar voice of Tomas Collins came on the radio. That's odd, Sam thought. He usually only works the Monday through Friday shift.

"As many of you know," the voice on the radio began, "I rarely work the weekend shift. But I felt I had an obligation to speak to you, the people of the greater Los Angeles area, and so I asked a favor of Bob McKinley, our station manager. I'm proud to say that he agrees with me that this topic that I'm about to bring up must be discussed with all of you now. So for the next four hours I'll be talking about a murder that happened in our beloved city of Los Angeles.

"As you heard at the top of the hour, a body was discovered in the home of Dr. Blake Covington yesterday. I spoke with a member of the Los Angeles Police Department last night and on the condition of anonymity, he gave me details of the scene that has not been released to the people of Los Angeles County. The true nature of this shocking crime is something that every citizen is entitled to know.

"The police know that there are at least two victims that were found in the home, not just one, as they have led you and I to believe. They are aware that the bodies were dissected with surgical precision, while the individuals were alive and conscious. They are aware that Dr. Blake Covington and his automobile are missing. They know that he is a surgeon with the skills needed to perform such a horrendous crime as this. They suspect that there will be others to die in this same fashion.

"So why is it that you and I have not heard this information from them? Are they trying to protect some madman because of family status and wealth? Are we going to have yet another case in Los Angeles where, if you have fame and fortune, you can get away with murder? Does the Covington Oil name buy police protection from prosecution in this city? The lines are open now. Tell me what you think. The number is eight, eight, eight, five, five, five, ten, ten. I'll be here for the next four hours. Call me now."

"Son of a bitch!" Sam shouted, slamming her fist into the dashboard, waking Junior up with a start. "How the hell did he find out what we know? Who leaked him that information?"

Sam listened for the next half an hour until they were out of range of the radio signal. Many of the callers claimed to have had personal experiences with Dr. Covington, all of them relating how horrible he had been to them.

As the static on the radio began to drown out any recognizable sounds, she called Jennifer Daniels, waking her out of a dead sleep. "Daniels," she said. "I need you to get up and turn on your radio."

"Sam, is that you?" Jennifer asked, still not fully awake. "Do you know what time it is?"

"Yeah, I do. It's time for you to get up and turn your radio on. Tune it to am 1010. The host is doing a four hour show about what the police know and don't know about this case. I need you to listen carefully. Try and figure out who leaked the story to them and listen for our killer. He or she might try to call in. Listen for someone who, as a private citizen, knows more than they should. Got it?"

"Yeah, I've got it. Can I at least grab some coffee first?" she asked with a yawn.

"Radio on first. Get your coffee at the commercial break. And take notes. I'll call you when I get to Modesto."

Sam hung up just as they were cresting the Tejon Pass, starting their descent into the Central Valley. As long as the road stayed clear they should arrive in Modesto by ten.

Junior woke up a little before eight. He looked over at her speedometer. It said they were traveling along at ninety-five. "In a bit of hurry?" he asked.

"I hate long drives. They make me cranky."

"Oh, so I've only gotten to see the soft, gentle side of you up to this point."

"Are you trying to get smart with me?"

"Would you prefer me to stay as dumb as you think I am?"

For the first time since they met, she had no comeback for him, so she did the only two things she could. She frowned at him and pushed the accelerator pedal down harder.

It was closer to nine o'clock when they arrived in Modesto. Sam took the Kansas street exit off of the 99 and they stopped at the little mom and pop café just off the freeway for some breakfast and a review of how they were going to handle the interview with Sister Margret Hudson.

14

"Thank you for taking the time to speak with us," Sam said, as Sister Margret led them to the convent office.

"I am always glad to help the police if they need my services," Sister Margret said in a stern voice as they entered the room. "I am just not sure why the Los Angeles Police would come all the way up to Modesto to speak with me."

"We're investigating…" Junior began, only to be interrupted by Sam.

"What we were wondering," she cut in, glaring daggers at Junior, "was, when was the last time you were in Los Angeles?"

"Oh, come now, detective. You and I both know that's not why you are here. My past travels? Nonsense. You are homicide detectives. Who got killed and why did you travel up here to talk to me about it? What makes you think I would know about the goings on in Los Angeles?"

"Do you know a Blake Covington? Or a John Porter?" Sam asked bluntly.

Sister Margret had a bemused look on her face. "No, I do not believe I do."

"We already know that you've been here for the past

few months. What we're trying to discover is how your fingerprints were at a crime scene in Los Angeles while you were up here?"

"My fingerprints? That is utter nonsense. How could my fingerprints get down there, if I were here?"

"That's what we're trying to find out, ma'am," Junior interjected.

"I'm not a ma'am, I'm a nun," she said, fully offended by his comment. "You may call me Sister."

"What my colleague meant to say," Sam began, giving an inward shutter at the thought, "was that your prints were found on a champagne glass at the scene of a murder. Do you have any idea of how your prints got on that glass?"

"I have not drank out of a champagne glass since Father O'Donnell's wake a number of months ago."

Sam and Junior both looked more confused than ever. This case wasn't making any sense. Sam was about to ask how he had died when Sister Margret asked, "Did this have anything to do with his murder?"

Lights began to turn on in Sam's mind. "Could you tell us about what happened to him? To Father O'Donnell?"

"There is not really that much to tell. The police came and did an investigation. They never did find out who killed him like that. It was so sad. Whoever did that to him was depraved."

Sam could hardly hold back her excitement that she might be on the verge of getting her first real break in this case. "Could you tell us, please, what happened to him?" she asked.

"It was disturbing. It was just a few months ago. He had gone out to get some supplies for the Easter decorations for the church. He was supposed to be gone for about an hour, but he didn't come back. By nightfall, I called the police."

"When did they find him?"

"Two days later. And I was the one who found him. I went into his private study because I thought I heard a noise in there. And there he was. Lying on the floor. It was so disturbing what they had done to him. How could someone do that to another human being? Especially someone as kind and loving as Father O'Donnell?"

"What had been done to him? What did you find?"

"It looked as if someone had tried to take him apart from his feet to his knees. The skin was all pulled back away from the flesh. And the bones and the muscles had been taken apart. It's not right what they did to him," she said as she started to cry. "And then if that was not enough, they stabbed him in the chest."

"I'm sorry for your loss, Sister," Sam said. "And I'm sorry to have to make you relive that horrible experience. Do you have any idea who might have wanted to hurt him like that? Who would do such a thing?"

"I told the officers to talk to that girl. She kept telling the police those lies. I would bet my life that she was mixed up in this somehow."

"What girl? And what lies was she telling?"

"That student at the college down there.""

Maybe you could tell us the whole story, so we can try to piece it together," Sam said gently.

"Oh, let's see. It had to be, oh more than a decade ago. Father O'Donnell had been asked to attend a church conference down in Norwalk. One night after the seminar, his Volvo was stolen. He did not know about it until the next morning. He reported it stolen, but by then it had been involved in a hit and run accident. Some people had been killed, and that girl swore that it was the Father that had been driving. He told me that it was not him driving and quite frankly, I believed him. But she would not let it go. She spoke to the police. When they did not do anything, she went to the church leaders at the seminar. When that failed, she went to the press. She tried to ruin that man's good reputation."

"Do you remember her name?"

"Oh, let me see. I think it started with a J. Julie? Jenny? Janie? Yes, that's it! Janie. Janie Woodssssssssomething or other. I do not remember. If the police did their job, which I doubt, her name will be in their report."

"Thank you for your time," Sam said, standing up to go. "One last question if I could please. Do you ever wear lipstick?"

"Me? Heavens no! Well except on very rare occasions."

"Were you wearing lipstick at Father O'Donnell's wake?"

"Yes, I believe so. Red. Ruby Red, I think it was called. It was his favorite color. I wore it in memory of him," she said.

"Thank you again," Sam said as she led Junior out the door.

When they got into her car Sam said, "Son of a bitch! We've got to get that report." They headed downtown to the police station on G Street. Five minutes later, they pulled into the parking lot and went inside to speak with the duty officer. Twenty minutes after that, they came out with the homicide report for the late Father Gregory O'Donnell.

While they drove around Modesto looking for a place they could agree on for lunch, Junior read the report aloud. It was as Sam suspected. Skin separated from the tissues. Burns on the flesh. On both legs from the knees down, the muscles had been scraped away from the bones. But something had gone wrong. The dissection had stopped at that point. Then, the killer had gone into a rage. The chest had been stabbed twenty-seven times. The autopsy report showed that while the dissection had been performed while the victim was still alive, the stabbings had occurred post-mortem. Father O'Donnell had gone into cardiac arrest due to the traumatic event, but there was no evidence that anyone had tried to resuscitate him. Then he read aloud the piece of information she had been looking for. Traces of vecuronium, succinylcholine and clonazepam in the blood. The homicides were connected.

Sam's mind was racing, putting this new information together. It wasn't until Junior had repeated her name several times did she realize he was speaking to her.

"Detective Franklin, did you hear what I said?"

"What?" Sam said, shaking her head as if to clear it.

"Here it is, just as Sister Margret had said it would be." Junior pointed to a spot on the page he was holding up. The name on the page was Jane Woodman. Blake's real estate agent.

Jane Woodman had a vendetta against the priest. But why did she think he was involved in the hit and run? She reached for her phone to call Jennifer Daniels when the phone rang. It was Jack Adams. "Talk to me, Jack," she said.

"I just thought you'd want to know. DNA results just came back. That was the doctor we found in little bits and pieces."

"Thanks," she said. "I appreciate it." She hit the end call button and then started to scroll through her contacts for Jennifer Daniels' number when another call came through. This time it was from Captain Erikson.

"Sam, give me an update on what we've got. Somebody leaked the story to the press. I've got to get a jump on this before it goes all ape-shit on us."

"Yes sir. I just got off the phone with Jack. DNA confirms our victim was Blake Covington."

"Aww, shit," Erikson said. "He was our best suspect."

"Yes sir, I know, but I'm working on a new theory. We assumed that it would have to be a skilled surgeon to do that to someone else. But what if what we found yesterday isn't the first kill? What if there were others, say, practice kills leading up to our killer being able to dissect someone alive? What if they worked out all the bugs associated with different complications associated with torturing someone to death?"

"Interesting theory. Do you have any evidence to support it?"

"Our conversation with Sister Margret. Apparently a priest, Father Gregory O'Donnell was killed in a similar way to what we found yesterday. The biggest differences being that the killer stopped at the knees, and then repeatedly stabbed the victim in the chest, postmortem, suggesting a rage. Perhaps the victim died before our killer could finish the job properly. Autopsy shows cause of death as cardiac arrest. Although there was cauterization on the muscles, there is no evidence of any attempts to try and resuscitate the victim. Maybe the killer hadn't planned on him having a heart attack."

"If you're right, then we may have a serial killer on our hands. One that has found a new and inventive way to kill."

"Maybe not, sir."

"What do you mean? Did you find anything else out up there?"

"Yeah. Blake's real estate agent? Jane Woodman? She had it out for Father O'Donnell. Apparently she accused him of hit and run where a death was involved."

"Okay, finish up in Modesto and then head over to Palo Alto and see if you can tie this Jane Woodman to the property manager. I'll get a hold of Sheppard and have her check into this hit and run. Then I'll have her send a request to other departments to see if they have had any similar unsolved homicides."

A thought reached out and grabbed Sam's mind. "Have her give me a call when she gets the information on the hit and run."

"Okay, I will. Now get over there and get some answers. I've already had three calls from the mayor today."

"Will do," she said and hung up the phone. She looked over at Junior and said, "Whatever we do for food had better be quick and we'll take it with us. We can eat on the road. We've got to get over to Palo Alto."

They went through the drive thru of the local burger joint on McHenry before heading to the 99. After an hour and a half of driving, they were in Fremont, driving past Newark, headed to the Dumbarton Bridge. Sam hadn't been back up here since she settled her parent's affairs. Although she and Leslie had agreed not to sell their parent's house, she wasn't ready to face going back into her childhood home. Not yet, anyway. As far as she knew, neither had Leslie, but then again, she didn't know for sure. She hadn't spoken to her sister in six years.

They drove across the Dumbarton Bridge, made their way through East Palo Alto and across the 101, and into the city of Palo Alto. They pulled up to the University Lane Apartments and went into the office.

15

It was no coincidence that the University Lane Apartments had been built in 1959, the same year as the Stanford Medical Center. It had originally been designed to house the growing number of medical students enrolled there. With two hundred apartments in a garden like setting, all within walking distance of the campus, it was the ideal setting for med students. Loud tenants and wild parties were not tolerated. Although an older set of buildings, the apartments had been well maintained, including a number of key upgrades over the years.

When Sam and Junior walked into the office the first thing they saw was a petite brunette yelling at someone on the phone. She looked frazzled.

"Well what am I supposed to do until then?" she screamed and paused for a response. "That's a load of horse shit and you know it. I need you to find a way. Don't give me any excuses. Just do it!" she said, slamming the phone down. She looked up and noticed the two detectives standing there.

"I'm sorry about that," she said with a frayed smile. "How can I help you?"

Sam held up her detective's shield. "I'm Detective Franklin and this is Detective Evans. Los Angeles Police Department, homicide division. We'd like to speak to the manager."

"Los Angeles? Aren't you a bit out of your jurisdiction?" the woman said with an attempt at humor.

"Are you the manager of this property ma'am?"

"No sense of humor," she said, almost under her breath. "Okay, yes, I am. Sophia Reagan," she said with a forced smile. "I manage this property and three hundred others. I'm a little bit busy with this being the first of the month. What can I do for you detectives?"

"We wanted to know what you can tell us about John Porter."

"Los Angeles? Is that where he is? You tell him he's fired and he's not getting any kind of recommendation from me. And tell him that he needs to come get his shit out of the manager's apartment. What did he do anyways?"

"I'll ask the questions here, Ms. Reagan. When was the last time you've seen Mr. Porter?"

"He was here to collect the rents and to run the day to day operations three months ago. He was supposed to call me on the first, the month before last. When he didn't call, I didn't think anything about it. Sometimes he forgets to call if something has come up, you know, like an issue with one of the apartments?"

"So when did you realize he was missing?"

"I didn't hear from him at all on the second, and when I went to check the bank records online, I saw that he hadn't made any deposits either day."

"Did that worry you? Did you think he had run off with the rent monies?"

"Was I worried about him? Yes. Did I think that he had taken the money? No. It would be a headache to track him down, but it could be done if he had taken any of the tenant's rent money. We have a standing policy here and we let all of our tenants know that we do not, under any circumstances, accept cash. Rent must be paid with a cashier's check made out to the University Lane Apartments."

"So when did you discover that he was missing?"

"I came over to see what was going on with him on the third. The office was locked and there was a bunch of rent checks in the drop box. I tried knocking on his door, but he didn't answer. I came back here to the office and let myself in. After I gathered up the rent checks, I examined the daily activity log. The last activity John had recorded was on the thirty-first. I called the police and filed a missing person's report. I had them do a wellness check. After all, John is in his sixties."

"And how did that go?"

"I let the officers into his apartment, and, after a few minutes, they came out and said that he wasn't in there. Legally, because he's an employee, I can't do anything with his things until I have confirmation of where he is. I've had to have someone down here every day for the last two months handling business that he should be doing. Today, I didn't have anyone else. I have to be here. And I'm still trying to take care of the other buildings we manage, while I'm stuck here. Do you know how hard it is to run a property management business when you are stuck at one property dealing with the day to day issues?"

"No, I can't say that I can."

"Well let me just tell you, it isn't easy. Anyway, I was on the phone with our attorney when you walked in. I was trying to have her find some loophole or something that would let us get his junk out of the manager's apartment so that I can get someone else in here. But now that you've got him… wait a minute. Did you say homicide division? Did John kill someone?"

"No, ma'am. It looks like Mr. Porter was the victim of a homicide."

"John's dead?"

"That's what it looks like. What can you tell us about him?"

"He's been with our company for more than thirty years. He's one of the best on-site managers we have… had."

"Then why were you telling me to let him know that he's fired?"

"Look, John *had been* one of our best on-site managers. He made sure the place stayed clean and maintained. He found a way to keep the problem applicants from applying and if one of the tenants turned out to be an issue, he got them out. Discreetly. And quickly. He was good at his job. He never asked for a raise either. Of course as the years have gone by, he always got a small increase in his salary, but I never could understand how he could afford all of the things he did not to mention the stuff he would buy. He must have made some wise investments over the years."

"What do you mean? What sort of things would he do or buy?"

"Well, like last year, about a week before the Super Bowl, he got tickets to the game. On the fifty yard line. He took a trip to Hawaii the month after that. Six months ago he bought that Mercedes of his. You know, things like that."

"Do you know if anyone had ever threatened him? Or had any reason to want to harm him?"

"You're kidding, right? A property manager of two hundred units? He was strict with the tenants. That's why we hired him. That's why he's been here so long. Between giving warnings to those punks that want to be doctors and that don't think the rules apply to them, and having to evict problem tenants, not to mention the students that are trying to pass through to get to the campus? Over a period of thirty years? Yeah I'd say he's made more than a few people upset."

"Is there anyone that stands out in your mind? Someone with a lot of anger? Someone who would hold a grudge against him?"

Sophia thought for a moment. "No, not anyone that stands out."

"Is it possible to get copies of any paperwork indicating who he came in contact with during his time here? Both applicants and tenants. As well as a list of those who he's had to evict?"

"Thirty years' worth? You've got to be joking. No way. Do you know what kind of work would be involved in getting that to you? Plus, I've got to think of the tenant's right to privacy."

Sam pulled out her phone and hit some buttons. Then she held up her phone with a picture of the leathered message board. "Ms. Reagan, this is what someone did to your property manager of thirty years. I need those documents," she said in a commanding voice.

Sophia turned green and looked away quickly, covering her mouth as if to stop the retching. "Is that? Was that? John?"

"Yes, ma'am. Now get me those files."

"I can only do that if you have a court order."

"Hold that thought," Sam said as she punched a number into her phone. A few seconds later a man's voice answered the phone.

"Sam, what have you got?" it said.

"Captain, I've got the manager of University Lane Apartments here and she says we can't look at the rental files without a warrant."

"Consider it done. Let her know it'll be there within the hour," he said and hung up the phone.

Sam hung up and put her phone back in her jacket

pocket. "Well, Ms. Reagan, that warrant will be here within the next hour. In the meantime, I'd like to take a look at the manager's apartment."

"The police have already gone through it two months ago. They didn't find anything. I was just in there a few days ago to replace the battery in the smoke alarm. That damn thing was chirping so loud you could hear it all the way in here."

"I understand that," Sam said. "But I'd like to be thorough in this investigation. I won't disturb anything. I just want to get a feel for how Mr. Porter lived."

"Fine," she said. "Wait here while I go grab the key." She went into the back room and fished around in the desk drawer for the key.

"Do you think she could be involved?" Junior whispered to Sam.

"I doubt it. She nearly lost her lunch when I showed her the picture of John Porter, and she appeared to be genuinely surprised to find out that he was dead."

Sophia came back into the room. "If you'll follow me I can take you there. The manager's apartment is building five unit A."

She led them down a cobblestone path past two buildings and up to the door of apartment five-A. She unlocked the door and said, "I really should be waiting for that warrant before I let you in here."

Sam stepped around her and pushed the door open

the rest of the way. As she stepped into the living room, she found the missing pieces of John Porter.

16

To Sam, there wasn't even a question. The eight jars in a half circle filled with the red liquid, the three piles that she knew would be the bones, muscles and organs, it all pointed to one thing: whoever killed Blake Covington killed John Porter. Even from this distance, she could see the cauterization marks on the flesh.

"Ms. Reagan," she called out. "I know this is a stupid question, but was this here the last time you were in here?"

Sophia stepped inside. "Was what here the last… oh my God! What the hell is that?"

"I'll take that as a no, it wasn't. Junior, get her out of here," she said as she once again reached for the phone. He gently grabbed Sophia's arm and led her outside. Sam dialed the captain again.

"Sam, the warrant is on its way. I know I said get this caser solved, but give us a chance down here."

"We've just found John Porter. Well, the bits of him, anyways. If we want to have any chance of having Jack look him over you need to get a jump on this and talk to whoever it is you talk to at the Palo Alto police department."

"You really know how to mess up a guy's weekend, you know that?"

"Yeah, I love you too," she said and hung up the phone.

While waiting for the warrant to arrive, she took a look around the room for what didn't belong. She knew that whoever the killer was, he had left a clue for her to find. He didn't have to leave that glass with lipstick on it, but he did. Why? Look what I can do. They were bragging. Look what I can do . So, what was here that didn't belong? She looked up and saw Junior opening up the refrigerator. You've got to be kidding, she thought.

"Hey, Junior! I really doubt that there's anything in there that's still worth eating."

"No, I didn't think there would be. But why is this in here?" he said, as he pointed to the inside of the refrigerator.

Sam walked into the kitchen and looked inside. She immediately saw what he was looking at. The refrigerator was empty except for one thing.

"Why did he keep his bank book in the refrigerator?" he asked.

Sam put her gloves on, picked up the bank book and opened it up. "More importantly is why does John Porter have a bank book for Max Colton in here?"

"Who's Max Colton?" he asked.

"I don't know. But I'd bet anything that John Porter didn't put this in here."

By the time she and Junior were finally able to leave

the University Lane apartments, it was already early Sunday morning. Sam had called Nina Sheppard to have her run a check on Max Colton.

The necessary warrants had been delivered. She had the documentation that they had needed. An understanding had been arranged between the captains of both the Los Angeles and Palo Alto Police Departments. They would be working a joint investigation. Palo Alto police would be conducting interviews with any potential witnesses and the Los Angeles crime lab would get the pieces of the victim for identification and testing. The coroner's van was on the way up from Los Angeles.

As they pulled onto the 101 leaving Palo Alto, it was Junior who spoke first. "Wow. Two scenes like that in two days? You really know how to show a guy the ropes."

"Just wait until you see what I've got in store for you next week," she said. They were both tired and feeling a little punch drunk. They headed down the 17 up and over Patchen Pass on the way to Monterey.

It was close to eleven o'clock Sunday morning when they got to the town of Seaside, and Sam could barely keep the car on the road. They had been awake for more than thirty hours and had driven all over California.

She pulled off at the Sand Dunes Road exit and pulled into the Dunes Inn. While she waited in the car, Junior dragged himself inside to get the card keys for their rooms.

If she hadn't been so tired, she might have noticed the black SUV that drove behind her. The black SUV with the Twenty-First Century Real Estate sign in the lower right hand corner of the rear window. It drove behind her, exited the parking lot and turned onto the freeway heading south.

17

SUNDAY

It was a little past eight o'clock Sunday night when Sam woke up. She took a quick shower, got dressed and went to the room next door, certain that she was going to have to drag Junior out of bed. To her surprise, the door to his room was open, and he was dressed, looking as a true detective should. He was sitting at the desk in his room, working on his tablet while speaking to someone on his cell phone.

"Okay, thanks for the update... Nah, we should be heading out of here soon." He looked over his shoulder and saw Sam. "Yeah, she's right here. Do you want to tell her?" After a few seconds hesitation, he said, "Okay, I will. See you tomorrow."

"Alright, what was that all about? And what are you going to tell me?" Sam asked.

"That was Detective Sheppard. I woke up about an hour ago. I figured you'd want to get back to Los Angeles as soon as possible, so I got myself ready to go. When I was done I called her to see if there was any new information that we should know about.""

And..."

"She checked on that hit and run from 2003. It turns

94

out," he said, looking at the notes he had scribbled for himself during the earlier conversation, "that Jane Woodman was set to graduate from the registered nursing program at Cerritos College. Her parents were crossing the street to meet her when someone in a Volvo drove through the intersection and hit and killed them. According to the police report, Ms. Woodman said that the driver stopped, got out of the vehicle and staggered over to the victims. He yelled at the lifeless bodies that they should look where they're going. Then he got back into the car and drove away. She claimed that he was wearing a priest's robe. She managed to get the license plate number. The police discovered that the registered owner was one Gregory O'Donnell. Father Gregory O'Donnell. They got in touch with Modesto police. They spoke with the church and learned that he was attending a conference in Norwalk. By the time LAPD tracked him down, it was the next morning. He said that he had been in all night and had no idea why someone would think that his vehicle was involved. He took the officers to where he said that he had parked his car..."

"Let me guess. It wasn't there?"

"Yeah. He said it was there the last he knew and he filed a stolen vehicle report right then and there. They found the vehicle later that afternoon in the L. A. River. It had been torched. When Father O'Donnell found out what had happened, he tried to reach out to Ms. Woodman, to tell her how sorry he was for her loss. The word is she about lost it when she saw him. She kept yelling, 'That's the son-of-a-bitch that killed my parents.' It was her word against his, and he had a witness that he was in all night."

"The friend that he was staying with?"

"Yeah."

"But he could have been lying to cover up for Father O'Donnell. They could have abandoned the car, torched it and came up with that story. Did Nina come up with anything else?"

"Not yet. But she's still looking. After I was done speaking with her, I called Detective Daniels."

"Did she find anything regarding John Porter? Or Max Colton?"

"Yes, she did. Up until about nine months ago they both had been receiving ten thousand dollars a month, via electronic deposit into their bank accounts."

"Until about nine months ago? Then what happened?"

"Max Colton was living in the town of Baker, out on the I-15. Police were called to do a wellness check on him nine months ago. They found him dead. It really shook the small town. He had a cut on the top of his right foot from his ankle to each of his toes. Apparently someone had tried to remove the skin from his left foot."

"What was the cause of death?"

"Twenty-seven stab wounds to the chest. There were trace amounts of the drug clonazepam in his blood, but no evidence of the other drugs."

"So what happened to the money being deposited into the accounts?"

"The next month, the deposits stopped going into Mr. Colton's bank account. But Mr. Porter's account started getting twenty-five thousand a month. Three months ago the deposit was for forty thousand. After that payment, there were no more deposits."

"Do we know where was the money was coming from?"

"Detective Daniels is looking into that. She said she'd call me as soon as she found out."

"All right. Let's get moving. We need to get back home. I've got a feeling we're going to be very busy when we get there."

They loaded up the car, and got in. She was inserting the key into the ignition when her phone rang. It was Captain Erikson. She pressed the talk button, put the phone to her ear, but before she could say anything Erikson said, "Sam, when are you getting back down here?"

"We're just north of Monterey now and we're about to get on the road. Why? What's happened?"

"Good. That will give you plenty of time to get ready for tomorrow. I've got a press conference set up for you at noon."

"Press conference? Why me? What am I going to say?"

"You're the lead detective on this case and we need to let everyone know that it's not Blake Covington killing people."

"You sure know how to make a girl's life fun."

"Who do you think I learned from," the Captain said as he hung up the phone.

Sam turned to Junior and said, "Get some sleep on the drive home if you can. We've got one hell of a day lined up for us tomorrow."

18

MONDAY

"I'd like to thank all of you for being here today," Sam began as she looked into the crowd of reporters. "I'm Detective Samantha Franklin, Los Angeles Police Department, Homicide Division. I'm the lead investigator of the murders that were discovered on Ocean View Drive Friday morning. I can confirm at this time, that we have DNA evidence proving that Doctor Blake Covington was the victim of a homicide, not the perpetrator of it, as it has been suggested by some. I can also confirm that there was a second victim found at the scene, John Porter of Palo Alto, California. At this time we are still investigating the events that led up to this tragedy, as well as the relationship between the two. I can confirm that this was a double homicide and not a murder- suicide as has been speculated. At this time, we have no reason to believe this is the work of a serial killer. We are continuing with our investigation and ask that if anyone has any information regarding these murders, please contact the Los Angeles Police Department at the phone number you see behind me. Now I will open it up for some questions, but keep in mind, I cannot discuss specifics of an ongoing investigation."

One reported did not wait to be called on. "We've heard that the victims were found mutilated. Can you confirm that?"

"I'm not going to comment on the specific details of an

ongoing investigation. Next. You in the purple shirt."

"Do you have any suspects? Or motives?"

"We are looking at several possibilities for motives. At this time, we have spoken with several people but have not identified any one person or persons as being a person of interest in this case."

The questions continued on for another thirty-five minutes, all variations of the same basic theme. In the end, Sam had managed to maintain control her audience and steer the press conference in the direction that she wanted it to go.

As Sam stepped away from the microphones, her cell phone began to ring. She saw that it was Jennifer Daniels. "What'd you find?" she asked.

"Sam, you have got to see this. I found the money trail."

19

Jane kicked off her shoes when she entered the door to her home, picked up her cell phone and turned it on. After a few seconds, it came to life. Ten seconds after that, her phone went wild. Twenty-four new voicemails. Thirty-seven text messages. Well, that's the life of a real estate agent, she thought to herself. Leave town Thursday, get back Monday night; what do you expect?

She opened up her text messages and saw that they were all from Suzie. "Where are you?" one said. "I need to talk to you NOW!!!" said another. They were all various forms of the same message. She was about to check her voicemail when the phone rang. It was Suzie.

"Suzie, what's up?"

"Jane, where have you been? Do you have any idea what's been going on around here?" She began speaking so fast, she became incoherent.

"Slow down, Suzie. I just got back into town. I had to celebrate that commission check. What's so important?"

"Blake's dead."

"What?"

"Yeah, and the police think we're involved," Suzie said.

She spent the next half hour filling Jane in on the details.

"So what did you tell them?"

"I told them what we'd said we'd tell them if anyone came around asking. That we both left the club around two. But like I said, someone at the club told the cops we left at ten. And then they told them that we had been fighting and that we were discussing killing someone. What are we going to do?"

"First off, no more talking to the police. They have a way of twisting things you say to make you look guilty. If they come around asking you any questions again, you tell them to speak with your attorney. Second, relax. They don't have anything on us. You know it and I know it. They're just beating the bushes to try and see what they can stir up. Take a deep breath and relax."

She hung up the phone and poured herself a glass of white zinfandel. It had been a long weekend. She was looking forward to getting some sleep. Right after a good relaxing soak in the tub.

She went into the bathroom and turned the faucet on in the tub. After a few minutes of filling up the tub, she poured some lavender scented bath salts in. She turned off the water, undressed and slid into the tub. Oh, yeah. This feels so good, she thought.

Twenty minutes later, she got up from the soak, rinsed off the salts, and stepped out on to the bath mat. She put her terry cloth robe on and wrapped her hair in the towel. She hated going to bed with her hair wet, but she just didn't have it in her to dry it tonight. The long drive had worn her out.

She drank the last of her wine as she walked into the kitchen and set the glass in the sink. I'll wash this up in the morning, she thought to herself as she turned the lights off and headed for the bedroom.

When she got to her bed, she pulled back the covers, preparing for the feel of Egyptian cotton on her naked body. She took off both the towel and the robe and started to get into bed. That's when someone stepped out from her closet and grabbed her from behind.

20

TUESDAY

BANG! BANG! BANG! BANG!

Sam took a step back from the front door and massaged the side of her fist. After a few seconds of waiting she stepped up to the door again.

BANG! BANG! BANG! BANG!

She took a step back again. This time she could hear a man's muffled voice getting closer.

"Do you have any idea of what time it is?" he yelled as he opened the front door, standing there in his full glory. "Get out of here before I call the police."

Sam held up her badge, unfazed by the naked man. "We'll save you the trouble. I'm Detective Samantha Franklin. This is Detective Richard Evans. We're looking for Jane Woodman."

"She's not available right now," he said. "You'll have to come back later. At a more decent hour." He made to close the door on them but Sam stuck her foot in the path of the door.

"We are detectives with the Los Angeles Police Department Homicide Division," she said slowly, enunciating every syllable while holding her badge up to his face. "I don't care who you are or what she's doing. I need to talk to her now."

The man paused for a moment and the yelled over his shoulder, "Hey Jane. It's LAPD. They say they need to talk to you."

From the background they heard a woman yell, "Do they know what time it is? Hold on."

A few minutes later Jane Woodman stepped in front of the doorway. She finished tying the belt on her robe, kissed the naked man and said, "Why don't you go put some clothes on, babe."

"Are you Jane Woodman?" Sam asked.

"Yes I am. Is there some reason you're pounding on my door at six in the morning?"

"Yes there is, Ms. Woodman. We need you to answer a few questions for us."

"About what?""

We just have some questions we need to discuss with you," Sam said. She decided not to mention any knowledge of Blake Covington, Father Gregory O'Donnell, John Porter or Max Colton. She didn't want to give too much away too soon.

"And for that you're pounding on my door at six a.m.? You're not even going to tell me what this is about? Come back at a decent hour," she said and started to close the door.

Sam put her foot in the door again. "Ms. Woodman, we can either talk here or we can do it down at the station."

"Am I under arrest, detective?"

"No, ma'am. We just have some questions for you."

"Great," she said with contempt in her voice. "Then I'll meet you down at the station at ten. I'll be sure to bring my lawyer. And by the way, Detective Franklin, is it? If you put your foot in my door again, I'll break it off when I slam the door on it. I'll see you at ten. You have a great rest of your morning until then. Bye-bye," she said and closed the door.

"I can't believe she just did that," whispered Junior as they turned and headed for the car.

"Shut up and follow me," Sam said in a low voice as she walked down the driveway to the car.

"What are we going to do?" he asked her.

"We'll get the black and whites up here. We'll let them know to keep an eye out in case she decides to make a run for it. Then we'll go grab a cup of coffee."

They waited for the first patrol car to arrive. As it approached, Sam walked up to the officer behind the wheel and began speaking with him. When she got back in the car, she started up her car and drove past Jane's driveway. She paid no attention to the grey Lexus parked there. Nor did she pay attention to the black SUV with the Twenty-First Century Real Estate sign in the lower right corner of the window.

21

"I'm Anthony Martin. Counsel for Ms. Woodman. Ms. Woodman informed me that you were harassing her earlier regarding the death of Blake Covington. There will be no more of that. You do not speak to my client again unless I'm present. Now, against my advice she has agreed to speak with you regarding the unfortunate demise of Mr. Covington. But let me assure you detective; this is not going to be a witch hunt. This is not going to be a fishing expedition. If I see you heading in that direction, I will end the interview and my client and I will walk out of here. Do we understand each other?"

Sam leaned into the table. "And let me make one thing clear, counselor. I'm conducting a murder investigation. I'm trying to get the facts. I will do everything in my power to see that whoever is responsible for this murder is brought to justice. Even if that means stepping on a few toes. Do we understand each other?"

They glared at each other for a full fifteen seconds before Mr. Martin said, "Fine." Then he leaned over to Jane and said, "I told you this would be a bad idea."

Jane replied, "I have nothing to hide. Let her ask her questions."

"Okay Ms. Woodman. When was the last time you saw or spoke with Blake Covington?"

"I haven't seen Blake since we put the offer on the house. As far as talk to him? He was on the phone with me every day until it closed."

"And why was that?"

"He was a control freak. Things were never good enough for him. Even when I found the house he eventually bought, even then he still wasn't satisfied. Do you know he actually wanted a three day close of escrow? Beginning on a Friday afternoon? He was impossible to deal with."

"According to the deed," Sam began, shuffling through some papers, "escrow closed on Wednesday, last week. Did you see him then?"

"No, thank God. I didn't have to be present for his signing of the paperwork."

"Where were you after escrow closed?"

"Stop right there, Detective," Mr. Martin said. He looked at Jane and said, "You don't have to answer that." Turning back to Sam, he said, "I told you this is not going to be a fishing expedition."

"Fine. I'll restate my question. I already know that you were at The Underground Carriage™ Wednesday night. I know that you were not alone. I know that you were discussing killing someone and that you had an argument with the person that was present with you. I know that you left there close to ten that evening, not at two, as some people would like me to believe. I know that you have not been heard from or seen since then."

"Was there a question in there for me?"

"Where were you between Wednesday evening and Saturday afternoon?"

"Nice try, detective. My client's whereabouts aren't any of your business. And it sounds like you have a lot of speculation and hearsay, but where's your evidence to support your accusations, Detective?"

"No, Anthony. It's okay. I'll answer this one. I was taking some much needed rest. I went to Vegas for the weekend."

"Do you have anyone who can corroborate that?"

"My client can provide evidence to support her whereabouts, if that is what you're asking."

"Okay, then let me ask you this. Who are John Porter and Max Colton?"

"Who?" Jane asked.

"Really, detective. We came down here to answer questions about the death of Blake Covington, and now you're asking about people my client doesn't even know?"

"Oh, she knows them alright. They were receiving monthly payments of ten thousand dollars each, until recently. Those payouts were coming from the trust account set up by her father. The trust account that she's been running since 2003. Then Max Colton died, and do you know what happened? The payments to Max Colton stopped, but the payments to John Porter increased. And they kept on increasing right up until his death two months ago. And then, almost as if by magic, those payments also stopped."

"And?"

"Oh, and there is the matter of Father Gregory O'Donnell. Please don't try and tell me you don't know him."

Jane stood up at the mention of the name. "That son of a bitch! He killed my parents! He got what he deserved! I'm glad he's dead!"

"Jane, sit down," Anthony Martin said, gently grabbing her arm and pulling her to her seat. "Your question for my client, detective."

"Did you kill those four men, Jane?"

"Okay. We're done here. Jane, let's go." They stood up and turned to leave the room.

"I could hold your client for twenty- four hours, counselor."

"On what, detective? All you have is speculation and circumstantial evidence."

"I have evidence that she was paying two of the victims hush money. Your client has offered no explanation for that."

"How's this for an explanation? Someone else was running the day to day operations of the trust. After a quick audit of the books Jane found an error in the payouts for the trust. She had the transfers stopped. A few months ago she noticed that someone had hacked into the system. Those damned computer hackers," he said with mock outrage, waving a closed fist in the air. "Not only had they reinstituted the wire transfer, but they had increased the amount paid out. There's your explanation. No plot to commit murder. Now drop this witch hunt or whatever you call this vendetta you have against my client. If you have evidence, hard evidence, bring it. Because the next time you even look at my client without it, I'll be on the phone with the mayor so fast, you'll be walking the beat, handing out parking citations before the end of the day. Goodbye detective. Let's go, Jane."

As the two walked out of the station, Junior, Jennifer Daniels and Nina Shepard all approached Sam. Junior spoke first.

"So, now what do we do?

"We find the evidence that links her to the victims. Nina, see if you can find anything indicating that Jane had more involvement in the day to day operations of the trust then she's letting on. Jennifer, see if you can get a judge to sign off on a warrant. I want to look at her office, her home and her car. The warrant should allow us to see if we can find any tools or equipment that would be necessary to dissect someone. Also, make sure the warrant includes looking for DNA evidence. And make sure it's a sealed warrant. I want to have a tracking devise put on her vehicle, you know like they did for that guy that killed his wife a few years ago? Junior, you and I are going to head out to Culver City. I want you to put some pressure on Suzie Brookhurst. See if you can get her to talk. If not, try talking to the secretary, Margie Rice."

"Got it."

"Will do."

"Good luck."

As they started to head in different directions, a thought struck Sam. "Hey wait a second," she yelled to the three of them. They stopped and turned back.

"What's up," Nina said for the group.

"We recorded that interview, right?"

"Yeah. Why? What are you thinking?"

"All of you, follow me."

They went into the viewing room where the interviews are recorded. Sam logged on to the computer and found the file that contained the interview with Jane and her attorney. She began to replay the interview at high speed until she got to the crucial part.

"...he killed my parents! He got what he deserved! I'm glad he's dead!"

"We didn't tell her or her attorney that Father O'Donnell was dead."

"So how would she know..."

"...Unless she already had prior knowledge of his death?"

Sam looked at the others and said, "Find out how she knew."

22

Sam and Junior were almost to her car when her cell phone rang. It was Jack.

"Hey Jack," she began. "I was just about to head out. What's up?"

"So you're still at the station?"

"Yes, but I was just about to leave."

"Good. I'm glad I caught you. Can you stop over here at the crime lab before you go?"

"You've got something for me?"

"Yes, I do. Come on back when you get here. Same table as before."

Sam and Junior backtracked from the parking structure to the coroner's building that housed the crime lab. "Dr. Adams is expecting you," the lab tech at the front desk said. "Go on back." She reached down and buzzed them through.

When they walked through the double doors into the back room, they could see Jack working on the table in the back. The pieces of the body that she and Junior had found in Palo Alto were now organized on the table for him to

114

examine. Sam called out to him, "Please, tell me you've got something really good for me!"

He turned around and gave her a wan smile. She could tell that this case was getting to him. He looked frayed at the edges. He looked tired. His gray hair was askew. He looked like he hadn't slept in days. Then again, she thought, we all must look like that.

"Yes I do," he said. "Several things, in fact. First, DNA confirms that these pieces had once been John Porter. We also confirmed that the drug mixture we found in Dr. Covington is present in Mr. Porter here as well. We also found this. Take a look under the microscope."

Sam walked over and peered through the lenses. "What is it that I'm supposed to be looking at," she asked.

"You're looking at the latest victim's somatic cells. Notice the larger than normal extracellular spaces and smaller than normal cells?"

"Okay, if you say so. What does that mean? In English, Jack."

"It means that, in addition to the victim's skin having been leathered, you now also have clinical proof that these tissues were frozen. Six to eight weeks would be my guess."

"That puts it right within our timeline of his disappearance."

"Hope that helps."

"It does. Anything else?"

"Yes, I've saved the best for last. In addition to the other similarities with Blake Covington's parts, John Porter's remains are missing his right flexor digiti minimi brevis."

"His what?"

"Seriously, Sam," Jack said with a sigh of exasperation. "When are you going to take a basic anatomy class?"

"Probably about the same time I get you onto a shooting range."

"So in other words, never. Fine. The flexor digiti minimi brevis is the muscle responsible for bending your pinky finger. It's missing. Let me stop you before you ask; it's unlikely that he would have kept it as a trophy. It's more likely that, with as small as it is, it got overlooked."

"So, where do you think it would be?"

"I don't know. It could still be in whatever freezer the body had been kept in; it could be in the vehicle that was used to transport the body. It's small enough that it might have been dropped on the way to or from the vehicle. But I'll tell you this. Find that muscle, and you've found whoever killed John Porter."

"And since we can tie Blake Covington, Max Colton and Gregory O'Donnell to John Porter, we'll have him for all four murders."

"So, you have been able to tie the victims together," came the voice of Captain Erikson from behind them.

"Looks like it, Captain," Sam said. "That is, it looks like

they were all killed by the same individual. But who he or she is or why they are killing these people is still purely speculative at this point."

"Keep on it. And let me know when you've got something concrete we can use."

"I will. By the way, how's Sean doing?"

"He'll be fine if we can ever get his asthma under control. His mother took him to the doctor's again today."

"I hope he'll be okay."

"Me too."

23

By Tuesday evening, it appeared the investigation had stalled. The four detectives were huddled around the murder board trying to establish links to the victims and the list of suspects. After several minutes of the four of them staring silently at the board, it was Sam who spoke first.

"Nina, have we heard back from any of the other departments? Have they had any unsolved homicides matching our victims?"

"I haven't checked since yesterday."

"Why don't you do that. And let me know what you find. I feel like we're missing something here."

Nina sat down at her desk and pulled out her laptop. After several minutes of typing on the keyboard, she looked up from her laptop. "Bingo," she said.

"Another victim?"

"Try two. The first is the police and coroner's reports from Roseburg, California. Nathan Carter, age forty-seven. Died eight months ago of a drug overdose…"

"A drug overdose? How is that related…"

"If you'd shut up and let me finish, I'll tell you."

They glared at each other for a few seconds before Sam said, "Okay, continue."

"Nathan Carter, age forty-seven. Died of a drug overdose. Large doses of clonazepam, vecuronium and succinylcholine in the bloodstream. Enough to make the heart stop beating."

"Anything else?"

"Yes. The chest had been stabbed twenty-seven times, post-mortem. The report says that he went missing eight months ago. His body was found in his home two days later. Then we have the reports from Healdsburg Police. Marcia Albright. Age forty-six. Both legs dissected to the hips. Cauterization marks on the tissues up to that point. Scraping marks on the bones. Traces of clonazepam, vecuronium and succinylcholine in the blood. It says she died from complications of shock. The chest had been stabbed, twenty-seven times, post-mortem. She disappeared four months ago. Her body was found in her home two days later."

"So now we have six victims?" Junior asked.

"Looks like it," Jennifer said.

"Look, I know this case is getting to us all. But let's keep focused. We need to find out what, if any connection these two have to Jane Woodman. Right now, we have circumstantial evidence tying her to four of the six murders, but that's not enough to make an arrest. Does the report say what they did for a living?"

"Let me check." Nina scanned the reports and said, "Let's

see. Marcia Albright, waitress. Nathan Carter, landscaper."

Sam rubbed her temples. "Let me get this straight. We have a doctor, a property manager, a priest, did we ever find out what Max Colton did?"

Junior answered. "He was retired. Former banker."

"Okay, a doctor, a property manager, a priest, a retired banker, a waitress and a landscaper. Different ages. Different sexes. Different areas of the state. Presumably all being hunted by the same person. What's the connection?"

Daniels said, "Revenge? Settle the score?"

"With as random as they all are, maybe they were just victims of opportunity," Junior added.

Sheppard said, "No. That wouldn't make sense. We're assuming that two of them were receiving payoffs. Large payoffs. That would mean that they would have something on Ms. Woodman."

"Assuming that she's our killer," Sam said.

Daniels added, "That's true. But let's not forget. She's made it clear that there was no love lost between her and Doctor Covington. As far as her ties to the priest, well, to be honest, if I knew someone had killed my parents, and gotten away with it? I might be tempted to take them out myself."

"But even that doesn't make sense," Sam said. "I agree, I'd want to go after the bastard that killed my parents. Especially, if I saw him do it, and then, he got away with it?

But wouldn't that be the end of it? I mean, even if I were getting blackmailed, would I go after the blackmailer or blackmailers with more vengeance then the person who killed my parents?"

"You wouldn't think so."

"Let's look at those timelines again." Sam took a dry erase board marker to a fresh board and drew a long, horizontal line. She then put twelve short vertical lines on the long line. "We have Blake Covington, murdered last week." She plotted a mark on the far side of the board and wrote his name. "And we have John Porter," she plotted a spot two lines before Blake's spot, "who went missing two months ago. Who else do we have?"

Junior piped in with, "Then there's Father Gregory O'Donnell. He was reported missing five months ago." Sam plotted the appropriate spot and labeled it with the Father's name.

Jennifer then added, "Max Colton went missing nine months ago." This was followed by another plot mark and name added to the growing board.

Nina said, "And now we have Nathan Carter, died eight months ago and Marcia Albright, four months ago." Sam continued to write on the board.

"So," she said, stepping back from her board. "We know that these victims are related. Even if we can't see how yet, we know they are. Our killer had a reason for leaving us those clues. I'm going to go out on a limb here, but does it strike anyone else as odd that there were no clues left that connect these murders until he got to Blake?"

Nina was the first to jump in with her insight. "What if Blake was special to the killer?"

Jennifer added, "But that doesn't explain how our killer knew all of the victims. Or why they were chosen. And in that order."

"What if we're looking at this wrong?" Junior asked. "We're trying to link how these victims are related to each other. You said it yourself, Detective. What if these were practice kills? Our killer wouldn't want anyone catching on to what he or she was doing too soon. It would make sense that they would be spread out like this. But if you look," Junior walked up to the board, "assuming Max Colton was the first victim. Our killer drugged him with clonazepam. What if that was enough to sedate him, but not enough to keep him sedated once the killer started cutting on him?"

The room at large seemed to go silent as they listened to Junior explain his theory.

"And a month later, the killer comes across Nathan Carter. He's prepared to keep him sedated, but is unfamiliar with the dosage needed and inadvertently overdoses him." He continued down the rest of the names on the board. "And with John Porter, he achieved his goal."

"And what goal would that be?" Sam asked, angry that it was Junior that had managed to formulate this theory.

"Isn't it obvious? To kill someone while inflicting the most pain possible. John Porter was the first 'perfect' kill. Once he achieved that, he could start taunting the police."

"And, he could go after his real target. Blake Covington,"

Sam said.

Nina asked, "But if that's the case, why are there these gaps when he stopped killing? Three months between Nathan Carter and Marcia Albright. Then another two months between her and John Porter."

"I don't know," Sam said. "But when we figure it all out, we'll have the answers."

24

WEDNESDAY

When Sam arrived at the station that morning, she was surprised to see Junior working feverishly on his computer. "What are you doing here so early?" she asked.

"I wanted to check on a hunch. If it pans out I'll let you know."

Sam's phone rang. "Franklin," she answered. "Yes, Your Honor... I'm aware of that, Your Honor... No, I wouldn't have sent her to you if I didn't believe she was involved, Your Honor... Yes, Your Honor... Yes, Your Honor... I will. And thank you very much, Your Honor." She hung up the phone. "Let's go."

"Who was that?"

"That was Judge Thompson. Jennifer Daniels is with him now. He's issuing a search warrant for Jane Woodman's home, office and SUV."

An hour later, Jane Woodman was in her office when she heard a loud noise. She went to the window and peeked out of it. "There's a tow truck hooking up to my SUV!" she shouted to no one in particular.

She headed for the parking lot, but before she could get to the door, Sam stepped through. "Jane Woodman?

I have a warrant here to impound your vehicle and to search both this office and your home. Officers are at your place of residence now, and are posting this same notice. Come on in, guys," she said over shoulder as she handed the warrant to Jane.

"Wait a minute! You can't do this!"

"Ms. Woodman, I'm going to have to ask you to step aside or I will arrest you for attempting to impede an officer in the execution of her duty."

Jane went to the phone. She dialed up the private number to her attorney's cell phone. He answered and said, "Jane, what's the matter? Are they harassing you, again?"

"They're taking my car," she said, as she wiped away the tears. "They're going through the office and they've got somebody at my home!"

"I can't believe the nerve of that woman," he said under his breath. "You stay there. I'll be right down after I make a few phone calls. I'll have her badge for this!"

Half an hour later, Anthony Martin pulled into the Twenty-First Century Real Estate parking lot. Jane was sitting on the edge of the raised flower bed, while silent tears streamed down her cheeks. She had a look of stunned disbelief on her face.

"Jane," Anthony began. "I want you get out of here. Let me handle this. Do you have anywhere that you can stay at tonight? Or, anyone who can pick you up?"

"I've called a cab. I'll stay in a hotel tonight."

"Good. When it gets here take off. I'm going to go find out what the hell they think they're doing. I want you to call me tomorrow. Sooner, if you need anything."

"I will," she said, reaching a hand out to touch his arm. "And thank you."

He gave her a sympathetic smile, turned and went into the office to confront Detective Franklin. Little did she know in that moment, that it would be the last time she saw Anthony Martin.

25

Back at the station, Sam, Jennifer, Nina and Junior were sifting through the mountain of paperwork collected during the execution of the search warrant. Junior looked at his watch, pushed the paperwork aside and logged onto his computer.

"What are you doing?" Sam asked.

"I started thinking about it last night. We know that the parts of John Porter were dropped in his apartment some-time between Friday afternoon and Saturday morning, right?"

"Yeah," Sam said hesitantly.

"What if the killer dropped off the parts just before we got there and waited to see what we would do? So, this morning, I emailed Detective Johnston from Palo Alto. I asked her to check and see if they had video surveillance at the apartments where we found the bits of Mr. Porter. She sent me a text while we were serving the warrant. She said that she'd spoken with Ms. Reagan and that they do have surveillance at the complex. She said she'd send it to me by four this afternoon. It's just after four now."

"Okay, let me know if there's anything there," she said. She turned back to the other two and asked, "Do we have anything concrete linking Jane to any of the victims? Proof that she ran the trust that paid off John Porter or Max Colton? Any receipts indicating that she was in Modesto, Palo Alto or any of the other locations around the time of the murders?"

Junior interrupted, "Jane drives a black SUV, right?"

"Yes. Why? Did you find something?"

"That depends. What's her license plate number?"

Nina began sifting through the paperwork on her desk. "I had that here a second ago. Here it is. California license plate number RE4LIFE."

"And does she have any window decals on her back window?"

Jennifer picked up her phone and scrolled through the pictures she took this morning. "Here it is. Twenty-First Century Realty complete with her phone number."

"Oh, you've got to come see this. She is so busted.

"The three detectives rose from their seats and went over to the computer and watched the screen. "The only video they have is on the main entrance. Although you never see the driver of the vehicle, look at the license plate and the logo on the back of the SUV."

Junior punched some keys and the video began playing. A black SUV drove out of the parking lot. Even through the grainy video you could make out the personalized license plate. RE4LIFE, it read. In the lower right hand corner of the window was a window decal. Twenty-First Century

Real Estate.

Sam's cell phone began to ring. It was Jack. "Jack, I hope this is important because I think we're about to make an arrest in this case."

"Jane Woodman?" he asked.

"Yes. How did you know?"

"Because we've just found the missing muscle in the back of her SUV."

26

A total of eight cars swarmed Jane Woodman's house. Sam directed several of the uniformed officers to various points around the house. She motioned for Daniels and Sheppard to the back, while she and Junior went up to the front door. When everyone was in place, she started hammering on the door.

"Jane Woodman! This is the LAPD! Open the door!"

Nothing but silence came from inside the house. Sam waited ten more seconds and pounded on the door again.

"Jane! This is Detective Samantha Franklin, LAPD. Open the door!"

Again, there was no response. Sam called out on her two-way radio, "Does anybody see any movement?"

"Negative!" came the response from Daniels. One by one, the uniformed officers all had the same response.

"Negative."

"Negative."

"Negative."

"Negative."

"Negative."

Sam barked out the next order, "Daniels, Sheppard, come around front. Everyone else stay in position."

When they came around to the front, Junior asked, "What do we do now?"

"We need to have someone watching this place, but we don't want to tip our hand as to what we know. I'll get some plain clothes officers up here to sit on this place until she comes back. In the meantime, Junior and I will wait here until they get here. You two, go pay a visit to Suzie Brookhurst. She knows something. Bring her in for questioning. When I get back to the station, I want her waiting for me in the interrogation room."

27

Sam burst through the door, slamming it behind her. Suzie Brookhurst looked up at her and, with an attempt at attitude, asked, "And just why am I here?"

"Sit down, now," Sam snarled at her. "I'll ask the questions. You've got a lot of explaining to do. For starters, like why you lied about what time you and Jane left the club. Like why you didn't bother to explain the true nature of your relationship with Jane. Like where Jane was over the weekend."

"I think I want to talk to my lawyer now," Suzie said, visibly shaken.

"Fine. Don't talk to me. Between the witness who will testify that the two of you were talking about killing someone, and another witness that said she heard you two talking about killing Blake Covington... It looks like the District Attorney will get an easy conviction. I hear he's going to be seeking the death penalty. Imagine, that needle. Slowly, piercing your skin, breaking through, all the way to the vein. And then, with a simple push of the plunger, all the way down... No more Suzie." Sam got up to leave.

"No, wait. Wait! We never said we were going to kill Blake. We were only going to teach him a lesson."

"Do you really expect anyone to believe that crock of

shit? You and Jane are going down."

"But I didn't do anything," Suzie said with hysteria.

"Are you saying this was all Jane's doing?"

"We talked about hurting Blake, yes. But hurting him financially. Or maybe by damaging his reputation. But we weren't going to kill him."

"I don't believe you, Suzie. You have a bad habit of lying to me."

"No, I swear! We didn't touch him!"

"I think that you and Jane had had your fill of Dr. Covington and decided to take matters into your own hands. I think with Jane's medical training and your assistance, the two of you did this to several people," she said, as she shoved two photos of the crime scene in front of Suzie.

Suzie turned her head and began to make retching noises. In between retches, she said, "No I swear! I didn't do that to anyone!" She began to cry.

"You're lying again, Suzie," Sam pushed harder. "And I'm going to make sure you pay for it."

"No. I swear! I wasn't involved! I didn't do anything to anyone!"

"Then tell me what happened after Blake's house closed escrow."

Suzie talked through sobs. "We talked on the phone.

We were complaining about what a terrible person Blake had been. We went out to the club. I suggested that we key his car, or dump paint remover all over it, but Jane said that wasn't enough. She was crazed."

"And where is she now?"

"I don't know!"

"You're lying again!" Sam shouted, slamming her hand flat against the pictures on the table, causing Suzie to jump. "Tell me where she is!" she ordered.

"I don't know! I don't know!" she repeated, tears streaming down her cheeks.

Sam's phone beeped, indicating a new text had been received. She looked at the phone, and after a ten second pause, Sam said, "Alright, Suzie. I believe you. I'm going to let you leave. But if Jane contacts you, you'll call me right away. And try to talk some sense into her. Tell her that she needs to give herself up."

"I will, Detective. And thank you."

Sam opened the door and called to a passing officer, "Officer Hanson, please escort Ms. Brookhurst to her office. She's free to go."

Three detectives came out of the viewing room completely baffled by the rapid change in Sam's demeanor. As Suzie walked towards the exit, Junior asked, "You actually believe her?"

"Of course not. That's why, while you were watching me

during the interrogation, I was texting Judge Hathaway. He signed the warrant allowing us to bug her office, her home and her cell. Once he signed it, I was texting cyber-crimes. Detective Michaels owes me, or should I say, owed me a favor. While I was in there, he arranged the wiretapping and bugging. Now, if Jane and Suzie talk, we'll know all about it."

"That's brilliant," Nina said.

"Now, knowing the captain, I think I should go prepare for the press conference," Sam said.

"What press conference?" Nina and Junior asked in unison.

It was Jennifer who answered. "The one he'll want Sam to give to let everyone know as soon as possible that we've identified a person of interest."

"That's right," Sam said.

28

Jane hadn't called a cab, as she'd told her attorney that she would, nor did she stay at a hotel. Instead, she'd called her fiancé. He wasted no time in picking her up.

They left Jane's office, got into his Lexus and drove away. They stopped off in Santa Monica for a quiet dinner, went shopping to get her some new clothes, and then, went to his hillside Calabasas home. When he parked in front of the house in the driveway instead of pulling into the garage, Jane asked, "Aren't you going to park in the garage?"

He smiled at her and said, "No, I've turned it in to my workshop. I don't have room for the car anymore."

"It's a three car garage. How big is this workshop?"

"It's big," he snapped, without the smile. "And I'm working on a major project in there, so don't go down there. I don't want you to get hurt," he added, almost as if an after-thought. His smile was back.

They walked up the stairs to the front door. He unlocked it and motioned for her to step inside. After he stepped in, he peered outside, looked both ways and slowly closed the door.

After putting the new clothes and some toiletries away,

they sat on the sofa and turned on the television just in time to watch as Detective Samantha Franklin identified Jane Woodman as the person of interest in connection with the deaths of Blake Covington, John Porter, Gregory O'Donnell, Max Colton and two others. "Don't worry," he said. "I don't believe for a second that you killed any of those people."

"Thank you," she said.

"But, out of curiosity, why do they think you had anything to do with those murders?"

She paused for a moment, not sure if she should tell him the full story. They had only been together for a year when he proposed.

She decided on half-truths. "My father had business dealings with Max Colton and John Porter. The exact nature of those dealings, I'm not sure about. I do know they ended badly. My dad kept them quiet by paying them off every month. When he died, they wanted the same from me. Or else."

"Or else what?"

"Whatever it was that happened between them, whatever dirt they had on him, it could have affected the business as an entity, not just dad. As regards Blake Covington, I'm glad he's dead. He was horrible. Do you know he actually thought I was coming on to him? Eww. Just thinking about him in a sexual way makes my skin crawl."

"Hey now, don't be getting any ideas about running off with some doctor."

"No, a radio host will do me just fine."

"You know I will."

That brought a smile to her face. Anyway, about Blake. Someone overheard Suzie and I talking about plotting revenge on him. As far as Gregory O'Donnell…"

"The priest?"

"Yeah, he was a priest. How'd you know that?"

"I must have heard someone mention it on one of the earlier calls."

"Oh, I didn't know anyone down here would have known him. Anyways, he killed my parents. Hit and run. He claimed he wasn't driving, but I was there. And he was drunk. I know it was him. I'll never forget that man. And I'll never forgive him either."

"So that's the connection. That's why they think you were involved. But what about the other two people that they named?"

"I have no idea who they are or why they would think that I would want them dead."

"Well, I don't think you want to kill anyone. But I have a very special show to put on tomorrow, so I need to go to bed."

"You do? What's so special about it?"

"I'll be defending you, of course."

"Well then, you had better go get some sleep."

"I said I was going to go to bed. I didn't say anything about sleep," he said as he picked her up and carried her off to the bedroom.

29

THURSDAY

It was a quarter past ten when Jane woke up. It had been a long night. She had needed to talk and Thomas had been there for her. She spoke of how stressed this experience had made her. She was afraid of not being able to clear her name. She was afraid of losing clients and her business that her father had built up. She was afraid of not being able to support herself.

He had listened to her talk on until three. He held her while she spoke, comforted her when she started to cry, and reassured her that it would all work out in the end. He spoke of what their life together would be.

It was a relief to have this man at her side. When the talking was through, they made love passionately, desperately, gently.

She reached for him in the bed and when she didn't find him there, she realized the sacrifice he'd made for her. He had the morning show from nine until noon. He would have to be there by seven. They had gone to sleep at four. He had to be running on no more than two or three hours of sleep, at best.

She rolled over, grabbed the remote to his stereo and tuned his show on. The show he had dedicated to clearing her name.

"… And just why do you think they would try to hide evidence, if not for their ineptitude and laziness? Answer me that," Thomas said to the caller.

For the next hour, Jane listened to him defend her, shouting her innocence to the world. She was pleasantly surprised to hear how much support she had from the community at large. Motivated by the positive response to Thomas' show, she decided to get up, shower and get ready to take on the world.

After showering, she got dressed and started to wander through the house. Thomas' show ended at noon. He always had staff meetings after that. He probably wouldn't be home for another two hours.

She left the bedroom and headed in the direction of the kitchen. When she got to the hallway, she looked to her right and saw the door that led down the steps and into the garage. He'd asked her not to go down there. But why? What was he hiding?

She tip toed over to the door, turned the handle and gave a gentle push. It opened. Jane stepped onto the first step. Before she could take a second step, a gloved hand reached around from behind her and covered her mouth, stifling the scream. A needle was thrust into her neck as the contents of the syringe were emptied into her bloodstream.

"You were warned not to go down into the garage," were the last words Jane Woodman ever heard.

30

FRIDAY

Miles Elliot opened his mailbox. He pulled out what the mailman had hastily shoved in. A small box addressed to his wife. No doubt it was something she had purchased online. A bill from the electric company. And a hand written letter addressed to him. From David Covington. He opened it there on the front lawn and read:

Dear Professor Elliot,

I'm not sure if you have heard the news yet, but my brother Blake was murdered last week. We are all trying to cope with his loss. It has been very difficult.

He always spoke highly of you. It seems you took him under your wing when he was at Stanford Medical School. I would like to ask if you could please deliver his eulogy. I know that he would have wanted you to give it. He was very fond of you.

I hope you don't think this too presumptuous of me, but I have taken the liberty acquiring a plane ticket for you. I'll have my driver waiting at the baggage claim area at the airport. I have arranged to have you stay in the guest house on our property. The staff will attend to whatever you need.

The funeral is planned for Thursday next week. Please reply with your answer as soon as possible. I have enclosed a self-addressed stamped envelope for your convenience·

I look forward to hearing from you,

David Covington

Miles took the mail into the house, dropped all but the letter from David on the couch and took it to his office. He pulled out a sheet of paper and wrote:

Dear David,

I am so very sorry to hear of your loss. Blake was a gifted student who was very dear to me. Yes, I would be honored to give his eulogy. I look forward to meeting you in person on Wednesday, next week.

I'm sure this is just an oversight, with so much happening in your life, the tragedy of losing someone as special as Blake and the many arrangements that must be made, but I noticed that this is a one way ticket. I am certain that by the time we meet, you will have this resolved.

Thanking you in advance,

Professor Miles Elliot, PhD, MD

He folded the letter, placed it in the envelope, and ran out to see if he could catch the mailman before he drove away. As it was, the mailman was across the street, getting into his vehicle. Miles ran over to him, gave him the letter and thanked him. As he walked back to his house, he thought, Blake Covington, murdered. Wow. I wonder who could have done such a thing.

31

SATURDAY

It had been a frustrating past thirty- six hours for Sam and the rest of her team. Suzie had attempted to call Jane several times, but each time, the phone had gone straight to voicemail. The detectives from cybercrimes had tried to ping her phone, but they were unable to find it. They said it might be turned off. An attempt had been made to re-motely turn it on, but they were unable to do so. "She must have taken the battery out," one of them had said.

By early Saturday morning, Sam was going a little stir crazy. She had looked at the murder boards, trying to make some connection, looking for anything that would jump out at her. She had logged onto her computer searching for any connection between all of the victims and Jane Woodman, but to no avail.

She decided to drive past Jane's house on the way in to work. Maybe walking around the house, seeing it, being there, might give her some new insight, some new per-spective that she was lacking.

When she turned onto the street where Jane's house was, the first thing she noticed was that there was no un-marked car anywhere on the street. The next thing she saw, as she drove up closer to Jane's front door, was that it was open.

She called dispatch and asked who was assigned to watch for Jane.

"Officer Davis," came the reply. "He called in to say that he was going to find a latrine. But that was over an hour ago. He should have been back by now."

"Call him and find out where he is. And tell him to get his ass back up here now. And I have a situation here. I need back up, I need more officers than him. I'm going to... oh wait. Cancel finding out where he is. He's coming up the road now. But get me some back up here."

Officer Duncan Davis pulled up to where Sam stood. He was being followed by Junior.

"Hi Detective, what are you doing here?" he asked, with a sheepish grin.

"Where the fuck have you've been?" Sam shouted only to be interrupted by Junior running up, waving both hands in the air.

"Hold it. Hold it. Sorry, Sam. It's my fault. I was having breakfast down at the diner when Duncan, I mean Officer Davis here, came in. We went to the academy together. I told him to sit down and have a bite with me."

If looks could kill, the LA Basin would have gone into nuclear meltdown. She stepped within an inch of his face and said slowly with a sneer," I am Detective Franklin to you. How dare you encourage and incite a fellow officer to abandon his post!"

Junior looked like he was about to wet himself. Officer

Davis tried to quietly ease back away from her rage.

"Hold it right there," she shouted at Davis. She pointed back and forth between the two of them. "I would love to bust you both down to scrubbing dog shit and bubble gum of the sidewalks of Los Angeles, but right now, I need you two dumb-asses to cover me and act as my back up. Do you think you can do that?""

Yes, Detective," came their simultaneous response.

Sam unholstered her gun and cautiously eased up to the front door. "Jane Woodman," she called out. "This is the police! Jane! We're coming in!"

Sam led the other two into the house. They cleared the house room by room until only the master bedroom was left. As they approached its door, the first of the additional units could be heard coming down the road, sirens blazing.

Sam kicked hard on the bedroom door and the wood frame splintered beneath her foot. She looked around the large room. There was a small sitting area when you first walked in. A row of shelves and curio cabinets filled with a variety of books, awards, jewelry and tchotchkes separated the sleeping portion of the bedroom from the sitting area.

Sam observed the room for a full five seconds. There was no movement, no sound. She cautiously stepped into the room. She eased past the chairs and around the cabinets and shelves, and then she got her first real look at the other half of the room. It was what she had feared, yet expected.

She peaked her head back around the row of shelves and cabinets. She looked at Junior and Davis square in the eyes and said, "Time to get your scrapers out, boys."

32

"Seems like we just had this dance, Jack," Sam said as the coroner walked into the room. "The scene is the same as before. Blood in the jars, the muscles, the bones and the organs laid out like before. But we have a new message."

She picked up the leathered skin so that he could read it. The new message read, "**THOSE WHO CAN'T TEACH**."

"Those who can't teach?" Jack asked. "What does that mean?"

"That would depend on the emphasis in which you read the message. 'Those who can't teach' versus 'those who can't, teach'. See the difference?"

"Yes I do. But this isn't the same as before."

"What do you mean?"

"These bones are much smaller. Look at the size of the muscles. Let me just look here," Jack said, kneeling down, pointing to the hip bones. "Just as I thought. Sam, take a look at this. Do you see the distance between the ischium bones here?"

"If you say so."

"The distance is wide. It forms an oval shape. The distance between a man's ischium bones would be more narrow, giving the appearance of a heart shape. This victim is a woman."

"Jane Woodman?"

"I won't know until I get this puzzle back to the lab. I'll start DNA testing immediately."

"Thanks, Jack," she said. She walked out of the room and down the hall to the sound of Captain Erikson yelling. She walked passed Daniels and Sheppard dusting for prints in the living room and into the kitchen where she saw the captain continuing with Junior and Davis.

"…most incompetent, dim witted, stupid ass, shit for brains thing, I have ever heard of. You were supposed to be watching the place for Ms. Woodman. You handed the killer the perfect gift. An opportunity to drop the body with no one watching. And what the hell were you doing? Catching up on old times with your good buddy here? Don't try to give me excuses! I don't want to hear it! Get out of here! Both of you. You're suspended without pay pending an investigation by internal affairs."

"Internal affairs?" Davis asked.

"Why internal affairs?" Junior asked.

"We have a high profile murderer in this city right now. It's been all over the news, if you haven't noticed. And you just walked away from your assignment? And you, Evans. Detaining him? No, they're going to want to know what your involvement in this case is."

"We're not involved," they protested.

"Do you think the media is going to see it that way? Now go home."

They turned and walked out of the kitchen and towards the front door.

"You're lucky it's the Captain you have to answer to," Sam said, as Junior walked past her.

"Bite me," came his retort.

"I don't eat dumb ass," she replied.

33

SUNDAY

"…dumb ass, stupid, son of a bitch. Seriously, how thick do you have to be?"

"Samantha, I know this case is getting to you. And I know how you feel about Detective Evans. But please. Sit down and take a deep breath."

"Darryl, you know that breathing technique doesn't work on me."

"Try it anyway. Humor me. Consider it an order from your old partner."

Sam glared at him for a second or two and then sat down, closed her eyes, and took a deep breath.

"Thank you. So, how bad did he fuck up?"

"He talked a plain clothes officer into abandoning his post for more than an hour, giving the killer a chance to do a body dump at the house that he was supposed to have under surveillance."

"Wow. Enormous fuck up."

"And the thing that really gets under my skin is, it's not

like there's some big secret. This is a high profile murder investigation."

Sam's phone began to ring. She made no attempt to pick it up.

"Are you going to get that?"

She picked the cell phone and answered, "Nina, what's up?"

"Sam. We've two more hits. Henry Jackson, age seventy-nine, from Fresno. Went missing seven months ago. His body was found two days later. The coroner's report lists cause of death as asphyxiation. He had traces of vecuronium, succinylcholine and clonazepam in his blood. There were twenty-seven stab wounds to the chest. Then there's Bryant Anderson, age forty-seven. He went missing three months ago. Two days later, they found his head and torso intact, including the skin where the arms and legs had been. They found the bones and muscles dumped carelessly in one pile next to the body. He had been stabbed in the chest..."

"...twenty-seven times," Sam finished her sentence for her. "Let me guess. Traces of vecuronium, succinylcholine and clonazepam in the blood?"

"You've got it."

"Where was he from?"

"Sunnyvale."

"That's not far from Palo Alto. See if you can make any

connection between Bryant Anderson and John Porter... Or Max Colton... Or any of the other victims."

"Okay," Nina said, as they hung up.

"New development?" Darryl asked.

"Two more victims that look like they're connected..."

Her phone began ringing again. She hit the answer button and said, "Jack, that was fast."

"I thought you would want to know. The finger prints on message board number two belong to Blake Covington. And DNA just came back. That was Jane Woodman in pieces."

"Damn," She said. "Alright, is there anything else?"

"Yes. Whoever dismantled your doctor also dismantled Jane here. But Jane was dead before he ever started cutting on her."

"How do you know?"

"Cauterization marks. On our last two victims…"

"You mean Blake Covington and John Porter?"

"Yes, exactly. On our last two victims, the burns, the cauterization marks were all over the muscles. The killer was clearly trying to stop the blood from flowing out at a rate that would cause exsanguination. But on the muscles you found yesterday, the burns are superficial. Not only that, but they didn't sufficiently cover the tissues. They wouldn't have stopped the blood loss. There can only be one conclusion."

"Jane was already dead."

"Yes."

"Alright. Thanks, Jack," she said and hung up the phone.

"More news?" Darryl asked.

"Yes. The latest victim was made to look as if she were killed in the same way as the others, but she was already dead when they took her apart."

"Now why would somebody want to do that?"

Sam thought for a moment. "He didn't want her to suffer. Our killer had a relationship with Jane. Maybe she wasn't part of the original victims our killer was targeting. Maybe she found something that linked... our... killer... to..." Sam paused for a moment. Her brain was racing with the implications of the new information.

"Sam?"

"Hold that thought," Sam said as she held up a finger to Darryl. She grabbed her cell phone and dialed up Jennifer Daniel's number. "Come on, pick up," she said, pacing the room.

"Detective Daniels."

"Hey, it's Sam. Who do we have watching Suzie Brookhurst?"

"Hold on a second… It's Officer Nunez."

"Have him bring her in. Or better yet, have him go talk to her at her house. Find out who Jane Woodman was dating. Call me as soon as you find out."

"You know I will."

"Can I talk now?"

"What? Yes. Sorry Darryl. It's just that, we've never questioned Jane's boyfriend."

"How do you know she has a boyfriend?"

"Trust me, I know. When we spoke to her at her house, he answered the door. The way they interacted with each other. He wasn't just a one night stand. They were lovers. And I let him walk away without questioning him!"

"So, it's not just rookie detectives that make mistakes? Is that what I'm hearing?"

She glared at him. After a slight pause, she asked, "So what are you saying I should do?"

"Do you think that your partner had anything to do with these murders? Honestly?"

Sam scoffed. "Seriously? No."

"Then he made a mistake. A big mistake, yes. But a mistake, none the less. He's your partner. As much as you need to know that he will be there to back you up, he needs to know that too. Trust is a two way street. Do what you can to get him reinstated. Punish him however you want, once he's back. But don't hang him out to dry with Internal Affairs."

Sam looked at him with both anger and disbelief. "Oh look," she said sarcastically. "My time is up. It's been great talking to you Darryl, but I don't want to mess up your schedule and take valuable time away from your next client."

"Nice try, Sam. But we both know that it's Sunday afternoon. I'm doing you a favor meeting with you today. If we hadn't been partners back in the day, I would have had you wait until tomorrow."

"I know. I know. He just drives me nuts with his incessant..."

"I know that. But you know I'm right."

"Fine," she pouted. "I'll go talk to Internal Affairs to see what can be done to get my *partner* reinstated."

"Thank you. And now, I have one other thing..."

Her cell began ringing again.

"Franklin. What have you got for me?"

"Sam, I've got the name of the boyfriend. It's Thomas Collins. You know. The talk radio host?"

"Son of a bitch," she said.

157

34

MONDAY

"You just wait until my attorney gets here. You had no right to pull me off the air like that. I was in the middle of my show!"

"Mr. Collins, you can wait until your lawyer gets here. But by not answering any of my questions, you get moved to the top of the suspect list."

"For what?"

"Murder."

"What, you've finally realized that Jane was innocent and so, now you're coming after me?"

"Jane's dead, as you well know."

"What? When?"

"Don't play dumb with me. You have a choice. You can talk to me now or…"

Thomas glared at her. "Detective Franklin, is it? I'll take my chances with my lawyer."

They locked eyes in a dead stare for a full minute until

the door opened up. "Detective Franklin. Why are you attempting to question my client without council?"

"Mr. Martin. I wasn't aware that you were Mr. Collin's attorney."

"I am. Has my client been placed under arrest?"

"No, we just have some questions for him regarding the deaths of several people."

"Then you will submit those questions to me at my office, in writing. And you need to stop harassing my clients. First Jane Woodman. Now Thomas Collins? Tell me Detective; do you have something against me personally, or just against hard working citizens that have made a successful life for themselves?" Turning to Thomas, he said, "Let's go. This interview is over." Looking back at Sam, he said, "I expect a formal apology to both my client and his listening audience. If we get that apology, we might decide not to file a lawsuit against you, the LAPD and against the city. Good day detective." He led Thomas out of the interrogation room.

Sam stepped out of the room, full of frustration. Captain Erikson stepped out of his office and called her over. "Internal Affairs will be grilling your boy in five minutes."

"Thanks Captain," she said and raced up the stairs.

35

TUESDAY

Sam was convinced of Thomas Collins' involvement in Jane's death, as well as the other victims. She listened carefully to his show for some hint that he knew more about the crimes than an innocent person should.

After the nine o'clock news ended, he began his program. "As many of you know, my show yesterday came to an abrupt halt when the police came in and dragged me out of this studio, as if I were a common criminal. They refused to tell me why I was being taken downtown and continued to harass me even after I requested to speak with my attorney."

"So that's the angle you're going to play," Sam said aloud. "The victim? Trying to get public opinion on your side?"

From the portable radio on Sam's desk, Thomas continued. "… with no consideration of how I felt after the murder of my fiancé by whoever this mad man is, running around our beloved city, killing people in the most horrendous way possible. And then, she had the nerve to accuse me of being that killer! Me, of all people! To Detective Franklin, I ask, why would I kill my fiancé? How is it that I'm supposed to have known Blake Covington? I host a show on talk radio. He was a skilled surgeon. Why would I want him dead? What possible motive could I have?"

"He's got a point, Sam," Captain Erikson said.

"We'll keep digging. There will be a connection. I can feel it in my gut."

"…based on that argument, I'm calling for the removal of Detective Franklin from the Los Angeles Police Department. Fellow citizens of Los Angeles, do we really need this kind of rogue cop, thinking that she is above the law? Hasn't our beautiful city had enough black eyes over the years? We cannot afford to tolerate this kind of above the law mentality within our police force. We still live in a country of due process, do we not? The lines are now open. Call me and let me know what you think. Eight-eight-eight-five-five-five-ten- ten."

For the next three hours, Sam listened to the pure venom that spewed from the mouths of the callers.

36

"Sam, that was pretty intense. Raking the department over the coals like that? You know the mayor is going to be all over my ass on that one. Give me something I can use to show that we're not just screwing this case up, left, right and center. What connection do you have to the victims?"

"Look, Captain. We know that he was the fiancé of Jane Woodman."

"Yes, but she's dead," he interrupted. "Tell me you've got more than that on this guy. Please tell me you're not asking me to go to the mayor with, 'He's the fiancé of one of the victims.'"

"We know that all of the victims are related. The drug cocktail to incapacitate them, the early attempts at vivisection, the stab wounds post mortem, the later successes all point to the same person. We thought it was Jane. The evidence appeared to support that. But when she turned up dead, in almost the same way, we had to look at the fiancé. Her death was made to look like the others, but there was no evidence of torture. The killer had to have a personal connection to Jane."

"If he's the killer, then why did he kill them? What was his motive for the prior kills? And why did he kill Jane?"

"He could have been going after the people who had hurt Jane. Maybe she didn't know what he was doing.

Maybe she found out what kind of person he is and he had to silence her. If we can link Jane to all of the victims, we can establish a link to Thomas Collins."

"So, while you're looking for this link, this "evidence" that will tie him to the other murders, what's your plan?"

"I'm going to go on the offensive. I've got a press conference in," she glanced down at the watch on her left hand, "twenty minutes. If he's as arrogant as I think he is, if he believes that he's outsmarted us, the way I think he does, then what I'm going to say should provoke him. It should infuriate him enough for him to make a mistake. In the meantime, I've got Daniels and Sheppard looking for connections between the victims. We've already established some connections, but we haven't linked all of them yet."

"Alright. It sounds like a solid plan. Keep working that angle. By the way, when does your boy get back?"

"Junior? "

"Yes."

"Today's the last day of his suspension."

"You know they would have hung him out to dry if you hadn't spoken up for him, don't you?"

"Don't remind me."

37

"I want to thank all of you for coming here today. I'm Detective Samantha Franklin with the Los Angeles Police Department. I will be giving to you a prepared statement to update the citizens of Los Angeles on the progress we are making in regards to several recent homicides, but I will not be taking questions at this time.

"I can confirm to you the death of real estate agent Jane Woodman. We believe that she has been murdered by the same individual who killed Blake Covington and John Porter. We do not believe that the murders are random, nor do we believe that the public at large is in any risk."

Sam decided to turn it up a notch. "We also believe that the murderer is slipping up. He is losing heart. What he had been able to do, he appears to no longer have the stomach for. He is a weak, small minded Individual who hides behind others. He has made several key mistakes, and that will be critical in the capture of this lunatic. Our profiler has even suggested that he may be impotent, and that these murders are some kind of response to his erectile dysfunction. We have a person of interest we have attempted to question, but he is refusing to cooperate with us in this investigation.

"We have no doubt that we will make an arrest soon. Thanks to his recent blunders and ineptness, the evidence we are gathering will be sufficient to make an arrest in a matter of days. Let me assure you, that this individual is of no threat to the community at large. He is a sorry excuse for a human being."

From across the Los Angeles basin, a lone individual watched the television as Detective Samantha Franklin stood before all of Los Angeles. "...weak, small minded individual... impotent... erectile dysfunction... thanks to his recent blunders and ineptness..."

"Now it's personal, Detective," he whispered. "Game on."

38

WEDNESDAY

Sam drove up to Junior's apartment to pick him up. He was waiting outside for her. He opened the door and leaned in to speak, but was cut off by Sam's gruff, "Get in."

He climbed into the vehicle and she hit the gas. The door was slammed shut with the force of her take off. She took the first left turn with enough speed that he was thrown into the side window. "You need to put your seat belt on," she said.

He buckled the seat belt with haste. "Look, I know I screwed up," he said.

"That's an understatement," she interrupted.

"Then why did you defend me to Internal Affairs? Why not leave me hanging?"

"You really are an idiot, aren't you? Didn't you ever stop to listen to me? For instance, on the drive up to Modesto? You are my partner. I need you to have my back like I will have yours . I can't ask that of you if I'm leaving you to face things like your meeting with Internal Affairs alone."

This statement seemed to shut Junior's mind down for a moment. Then he asked, "Then why did you have to tow my car?"

"Hey that vehicle had eighteen unpaid parking tickets. Some dating back more than ten years."

"My car is two years old."

"I'm still trying to figure out how you managed to get parking tickets when you were twelve. You're lucky you weren't cited for driving without a license and without insurance."

"So are you seriously going to make me wait the thirty days to get my car back?"

"That depends on you, now doesn't it. Act like a detective and pull your head out of your ass and you might get it back sooner. Pull another stunt like that last one, and your car just might get auctioned off…"

"You wouldn't dare."

"…or," she hesitated. "It might accidently get sent to the crusher…"

"Oh, hell no. Come on S…" he caught himself just in time.

She raised an eyebrow at him.

He took a deep breath and said, "Detective Franklin, there will be no further reason for you to have ill will towards my person or my vehicle."

"Look out. You're starting to sound like a lawyer."

"What you did to my car was mean, but now you're getting nasty."

She drove them into the parking structure shared by the police station and the crime lab. They went upstairs and began to try and link all nine victims to Thomas Collins.

39

Miles Elliot stepped out past the secured portion of Los Angeles International Airport terminal and over to the baggage claim area. As a group of travelers walked in front of him, he began looking around for carousel number four.

He took his suitcase and garment bag off of the carousel and began to leave the baggage claim area when he noticed a man dressed in a suit. It was an all-black suit, complete with a white shirt and a black tie. He wore dark sunglasses and a black hat. His black leather gloved hands held up a small sign that read "Miles Elliot".

This must be the limo driver that David had said he would send for me, he thought to himself. He approached the man and said, "I'm Miles Elliot. I believe you are looking for me."

"Good afternoon, Professor Elliot," the man said. "My name is Terrance. I have been instructed to be your driver during your stay in Los Angeles. May I take your bags, sir?"

"Thank you, Terrance."

"If you will just follow me we can be on our way." He took the luggage from Miles and led him outside to the waiting black Lincoln Town Car Limousine.

"Looks like David knows how to welcome his guests."

"Yes sir, he does," Terrance said holding open the door. "If you would please sir." He motioned for him to get inside.

After Miles entered the limo, Terrance closed the door, loaded the luggage into the trunk and went around to the driver's door. He looked around to see if anyone had paid more than a casual glance in their direction. Certain that no one had, he got into the limo and drove away.

"Our journey today is seventeen miles, but with traffic we will be between thirty to forty-five minutes, sir. Please help yourself to a refreshing beverage. After such a flight as yours, you must be thirsty. We have water, juice, sodas and a variety of alcoholic beverages for your discriminating taste. Ice cubes are in the console to your left."

Miles took a few minutes and made himself a high-ball. Then, as he sat back in the seat he took the first sip. After a flight like that, this cold drink really hit the spot. When he had consumed most of the drink, he pulled out his phone and dialed his wife. It went to voicemail.

"Patricia, I made it down here just fine. Other than the screaming child back in coach, there weren't any problems on the flight." He began to rub his temples. "You know how I hate screaming brats. I think I'm getting a headache from that kid. Thank God I had a few drinks on the flight down here." He paused long enough to finish off his drink. "Terrance here picked me up. We're headed to David Covington's house. I'll call you after the funeral tomorrow," he said and hung up the phone.

He began to pour himself another drink, when he poured half the lemon-lime soda all over the front of his pants. "I say, Terrance. I don't quite know what happened, but I seem to have had an accident back here."

"Don't worry about a thing Professor. I'll clean it all up later," Terrance said in a soft, gentile voice.

Miles looked around and found some napkins next to the ice. After he took a few minutes to clean himself up, he finished preparing his drink. He took a sip of the fresh drink when the wave of vertigo hit. "Are we in an earthquake?" he asked.

"No, Professor. There's no earthquake. Did you make the drink a little too strong?"

"Terrrance, iss itt?" He began slurring his words. "How darre youuu asp mee about myy drnikink habbbhahits."

"Relax, professor. You're going to go to sleep now. Soon, you'll get to be with your old friend Blake."

"Hoow doo youu knew Blike?"

"I could never, ever forget you, Professor. Nor could I forget Blake. And professor? I could never forgive, either. Ever," he hissed.

40

THURSDAY

"Okay, let's go through this one more time," Sam said.

"You can go through it again all you want," Nina said. "But other than the priest, the banker, the property manager and the doctor, there's no connection to Jane Woodman or Thomas Collins."

"Well, we know that whoever killed them killed the other victims as well. If you have any other ideas, I'm open to suggestions. But I still want to go over this list again. I know that we're missing something here. Junior, go through the list again, in chronological order."

"If you say so," he said.

The strain of this case was beginning to take its toll on the four of them.

"As best as we can piece together, Max Colton, age seventy-three, was victim number one. He had been a banker before he retired twenty years ago. He disappeared nine months ago. He lived in Baker, California.

"Nathan Carter, age forty-seven, landscaper. He disappeared eight months ago. He lived in Roseburg.

"Henry Jackson, age seventy-nine, retired third grade teacher. He disappeared seven months ago. He lived in Fresno.

"Gregory O'Donnell, age fifty-two, Priest. He disappeared five months ago…"

"Wait a minute," Sam interrupted. "Our murderer has been killing one a month since he started nine months ago. Where's the victim from six months ago?"

"Maybe he took a month off?" Daniels suggested.

"Or maybe we haven't found the victim from six months ago yet," Sam said. "Nina, update our inquiry with the other departments state wide. We need to find a murder that took place six months ago." She turned towards Junior and said, "Go on."

"Gregory O'Donnell, age fifty-two, Priest. He disappeared five months ago. He lived in Modesto.

"Then there's Marcia Albright, age forty-four. She was a waitress. She disappeared four months ago. She lived in Healdsburg.

"Bryant Anderson, age forty-six. Physical trainer. He disappeared three months ago.

"Then we get to John Porter, aged sixty-four. He went missing two months ago. He was a property manager from Palo Alto.

"Next is the one we found two weeks ago. Blake Covington, age forty- seven. He was the Chief Surgeon at Cedar- Sinai. He went missing two weeks ago. Lived in between Malibu and Santa Monica.

"Jane Woodman, age thirty-eight, real estate agent went missing last week. We found her..."

Sam glared at Junior.

"Okay, *you* found her four days ago in her Beverley Hills home."

It was Daniels who spoke next. "If the property manager was killed two months ago, and Blake was killed two weeks ago, are we going to be looking for someone murdered last month?"

"I doubt it," Sam said. "If you look at each of these victims prior to Blake Covington, They were the practice kills. With each of the murders, our killer got closer to his goal. With John Porter, he succeeded in doing just that. A complete vivisection leading to death. That tells me that Blake was someone special. He was practicing to be able to kill Blake in this way."

Sheppard added, "That would be why the message, 'Look what I can do.'"

"Yes," Sam said. "He's taunting us. And the message he left at Jane Woodman's home, 'Those who can't, teach.' I'd bet money that we were given a clue as to who the next victim is going to be. He's going to kill a teacher of some kind."

Junior began frantically typing on his computer.

"What's up?" Sam asked.

"Just a hunch. Give me just… a… Bingo!"

"What?" Sam asked in frustration.

"Henry Jackson was a third grade teacher for the Fresno Unified School District. Guess who was a student of his back in 1976?"

"Who?" the three asked at the same time.

"None other than Nathan Carter, landscaper, most recently residing in Roseburg, California. According to our timeline, he would have been the second one killed."

Sam jumped up and ran over to Junior's computer, nearly knocking him over as she tried to get in front of the screen. "You know what this means, right?"

"We've connected two of the victims?"

"It means that these weren't just random strangers he practiced on. There's a connection here. All of these victims are related. We need to find out how."

41

FRIDAY

By late Friday afternoon, the four detectives had made headway in connecting the victims. Nathan Carter was in Henry Jackson's third grade class in the mid-1970s.

Max Colton, John Porter and Steve Woodman had been partners in a land development deal in Montebello in the late 1980s when the financial market had crashed. Through some unethical business dealings, they had managed to come away unscathed, although Steve Woodman had come out more unscathed financially than his partners had. The payouts to Max Colton and John Porter had begun in June of 1990.

Bryant Anderson and Marcia Albright had been dating briefly in high school in Modesto, where Father Gregory O'Donnell had led services at the St. Paul's Catholic Church on Coffee Street. They hadn't yet made any other connection between the three, but they were working on it.

And of course, Jane Woodman was the real estate agent for Blake Covington. And since John Porter's skin was found, along with the wine glass linking Father O'Donnell's murder at the scene of Blake's homicide, seven of the nine were definitely connected, and Sam was certain that it would only be a matter of time before they could link the other two victims to this killer.

Sam was beginning to doubt her instinct. She had been certain that it was Thomas Collins that had killed Jane, but aside from her, he appeared to have no connection to the victims. "Maybe we should revisit David Covington. Or Justin Wilde," she said.

"The doctor? His alibi checks out. And David Covington has lawyered up and won't talk to us. And Mister Dixon has made it clear. He will pursue a lawsuit if we start questioning David without some hard evidence," Daniels said.

"I know. It's just that…"

Sam was interrupted by the ringing of the telephone on her desk. Strange. No one ever calls this number, she thought. Everyone knows to call my cell. She picked up the phone. "This is Detective Samantha Franklin," she said into the receiver.

"Hello, Detective Franklin, you said? The officer I just spoke with transferred me to you. He said you could help me with my husband. I haven't heard from him since Wednesday, and I don't know where he is."

"I'm sorry, but who is this?"

"I'm Patricia. Patricia Elliot. And I was hoping you could help me. I'm trying to find my husband, Miles."

"As much as I would like to help you, Mrs. Elliot, this is Homicide Division, not missing persons."

"Well the officer I spoke with said I should talk with you."

"Really? Why would he do that?"

"I don't know. All I said is that my husband caught a flight from San Francisco to LAX two days ago. He called me to say that David Covington's driver had picked him up and that he would call me after the eulogy."

Ice ran through Sam's veins. "Mrs. Elliot, what does your husband do for a living?"

"He was the Dean of the School of Medicine at Stanford."

"And what did he do before? Before he was the Dean?"

"He taught Gross Anatomy there at Stanford for forty years. Has something happened to Miles? Is he okay? Your homicide. Oh my God!"

"Mrs. Elliot, please calm down. We haven't found your husband. He wasn't the victim of a homicide." Not yet, anyways, she thought. "Maybe you can start over and tell me what you know. You said that he was invited to a eulogy?"

"Yes, to give the eulogy for Blake Covington. His brother David sent Miles a letter asking him to give it. Blake was a student of his many years ago. It was such a shock to Miles to hear that he had been murdered."

Sam cupped her hand over the phone. "Junior, run a check and find out when Blake Covington's funeral services were."

A few seconds later, Junior looked up from the screen and said, "Saturday. Six days ago."

Sam took her hand off the receiver and said, "Mrs. Elliot? Do you have that letter that David sent your husband?"

"Yes, it's right here." Through the phone Sam could here paper being shaken in the air.

"Can you fax that letter to me? It might be crucial in finding your husband."

Mrs. Elliot agreed to fax a copy of the letter to Sam. After exchanging phone and fax numbers and many reassurances, they hung up.

"I know what the message means," Sam said.

"Those who can't, teach?" Daniels asked.

"What's it mean?" Sheppard asked.

"Listen to this," Sam said as she launched into a review of the conversation she had just had.

42

David fixed himself a second whiskey sour. It had been a hard last few weeks. Between learning that the company that his grandfather had started in the '20s had been sold and then renamed, and then losing his job, those things were bad enough. But to find out that he was a suspect in his own brother's murder investigation? The pressure was getting to him.

When he heard the music starting up, letting him know that the game was coming back from the commercial break, he headed towards the living room to rejoin the game. As he entered the living room, the front door flew inward, and the door jams splintered under the heavy kick of Samantha Franklin.

Immediately twenty officers in heavy tactical gear stormed in barking orders.

"Hands in the air!"

"Get down on the ground!"

"Do it now!"

As if nothing out of the ordinary had happened, David asked, "What the hell do you think you're doing, Detective?" An officer quickly pulled his hands behind his back and cuffed him before throwing him to the ground. "That's police brutality, Detective. "I'm sure my attorney will want to hear about this."

"Where is he, David?" Sam shouted at him.

"Where's who?" he shouted back. "My attorney?"

"Don't be stupid. We will find him. You'd better hope and pray that when we do he doesn't look the way Blake did when we found him. Check the house."

"Sam," Sheppard shouted from across the room. "Guest house. In the back. Just like the letter said."

From upstairs Sam could hear the repeated cries of "Clear" from one room after another. Sam walked over to where David lay, face down on the granite floor. "Is he in the guest house, David?"

"I don't know what you're talking about. Nobody's in the guest house."

"If that's how you want to play it, that's how we'll play it. Guys! We've got a door to kick in."

From the floor David yelled, "You don't have to kick it in. There's a spare key under the piece of obsidian in the flower bed next to the door."

Sam led the group out the house, through sliding glass door, into the back yard and up the path to the guest house. Junior turned the piece of obsidian over to reveal a lone house key. He picked it up and handed it to Sam. She took the key to the door, turned the latch over and opened the door.

Sam entered the door first, with her weapon drawn. At the end of the foyer was the hallway. Using silent commands, she motioned for two of the uniformed officers to check out the bedrooms. She and Junior moved noiselessly into the living room.

In front of the fireplace, were the pieces of Miles Eliot. A cursory glance was enough to know that the new message board was Jane Woodman. Carved into her skin were the words "**NOW ITS PERSONAL SAMANTHA**."

43

Sam stood outside the two way glass of the interrogation room, staring in. She needed to play her cards right. David hadn't asked for his lawyer; yet. She received the fax from Patricia Elliot just before seven. It clearly showed that David had lured Miles down to Los Angeles. His body was found in David's guest house. It was only a matter of time before she could connect the victims to David. They had already connected the victims to each other... Well, most of... They had already connected most of the victims to each other. If she could get a confession out of David, maybe it would make sense.

She opened the door to the interrogation room and stepped inside. She walked over to the table and put a thick file down. "Hello David," she said in a calm voice. Can I get you anything before we get started? Water? Soda?"

"Detective, is that what they did to Blake?"

"Yes David. That's exactly how we found Blake. But you already knew that, didn't you?"

"Are you high? What makes you think I could do that? I don't have surgical skills. I was a business major. I ran an oil company. Remember?"

"David," Sam said softly. "You don't have to play anymore. We know what Blake did to you. He sold your heritage. He never cared about your father, but you did."

"That's right, he didn't. But I didn't kill him."

"David, we can link Miles to Blake. And we can link Blake to the nine other victims. And we can link you to Miles."

"What are you talking about? I don't even know who Miles is? And what do you mean nine other victims? Are you telling me that this person, the one that killed Blake, killed nine other people in the same way?"

Sam was getting tired of the charades. She slammed both hands, palms out onto the table. "Listen, David. No more games. We found Miles Elliot's body in your guest house. We have the letter you sent him, luring him down here."

"How stupid do you think I am, Detective? Do you honestly think I would do that to someone and then leave the body on my property where it could be found so easily? And what letter are you talking about?"

Sam opened the file and pulled the photocopied letter out. She slid it across the table for him to see.

"This isn't even my handwriting! I don't know who sent this, Detective, but it wasn't me. And if you don't have anything else, I'd like to leave now. And I'd like to know who's going to pay to replace my front entryway?" He stood up, holding out his cuffed hands.

"Actually, David, I have some more questions for you. Sit down."

"In that case Detective, I'd like to invoke my right to have my attorney present."

44

Within twenty minutes of getting the call from David Covington, Will Dixon walked into the police station. Inside of ten minutes after his entrance, he was leading David out. As they walked from the interrogation room to their desks, it was Junior who broke the silence.

"Do you think it was him? Do you really think he's our killer?"

"He does have motive," Sam said. "But the handwriting clearly isn't a match."

"But the pieces of the body were in the guest house," Nina said.

"Yes, but the vivisection wasn't performed there. If David were the murderer, why would he have staged the scene in his guest house for us to find?" Sam asked.

"Maybe he's trying to throw us off? Maybe he's trying to make it look like he's being set up when in reality he's our murderer?" suggested Daniels.

"No, David's not that smart. And remember, we wouldn't have even known about his guest house or Miles Elliot, if we hadn't been contacted by Mrs. Elliot."

"Have you considered that maybe David was holding

the pieces there until he could figure out where to leave them?" Junior asked.

"That's an unlikely scenario. Whoever is killing these people is leaving us a message. He's taunting us. When he leaves a scene for us to find, everything is placed ritualistically. If what we found tonight were a staging ground, the parts, the blood in the jars, the leathered skin; all of those pieces would likely have been piled just anywhere. No, they were placed in their exact location for us to find. That guest house was the intended scene as our murderer wanted us to find it."

As they reached their desks, Detective Sheppard sat down and began typing away at her keyboard. After a few moments, she looked up from the screen of her computer. "Sam, I just got a hit on the missing victim."

"What? Who was it? Where is the victim from?" In her excitement she almost leapt over the desk to see who the missing victim was.

"We have a hit from the Stockton Police Department. The woman's name was Pricilla Carson, age sixty-eight. She went missing six months ago, just like you said. They found her body two days later. Her left foot was partially dissected. The skin on the top of her foot had been sliced from just above her ankle down to each of her toes. It had been pulled away from the flesh and was still connected to the leg when they found her. She had twenty-seven stab wounds to her chest, post-mortem."

"Did the medical examiner determine a cause of death?"

"He has cause of death listed as exsanguination. But he

also listed our drug cocktail of vecuronium, succinylcholine and clonazepam in her blood."

Sam's phone began to ring. She looked down and saw that it was Jack Adams. "Jack, that was quick. What did you find?"

"The finger prints came back on the latest skin. I'm sure it'll be no surprise to anyone to find out that we have a match to Jane Woodman."

"No, I'm not surprised. The pattern fits. Do we know yet if the latest pieces belong to Miles Elliot or not?"

"I won't know for sure until we get the DNA results back. However, the preliminary exam of the victim indicates that the distance between the ischium bones is narrow, giving the appearance of a heart shape opening. Your victim was a male, and he suffered from osteopenia. Together with the multiple locations of bone remodeling, I'd say that it's safe to assume that the victim was in his eighties."

"Miles Elliot was eighty-four."

"I'll know for sure by tomorrow when the DNA results come back. Oh, and one other thing, Sam. His right hamate bone is missing. I'll save you the trouble of having to ask. It's one of his wrist bones. It's possible it was kept for a future opportunity to plant evidence, like we found with the muscle that was placed in Jane Woodman's SUV."

"Alright, thanks," she said.

So in all probability, we've found Miles Elliot tonight. I'll need to call his wife. That's one phone call I'm not looking forward to having to make, she thought.

She turned back towards the group and asked, "Where were we?"

"Our victim from six months ago. Pricilla Carson."

"Right. So they found her at home?"

"No they found her at her job."

"Her job? Where did she work at?"

"She was a secretary for St. Thomas' Catholic Church in Stockton."

"Stockton's not that far from Modesto," Sam said. "Did she ever have any dealings with Father O'Donnell?"

Nina began tapping away at the keys on her keyboard. "According to what I can see, she lived in Modesto from 1977 to 1984. She went to St. Paul's Catholic Church on Coffee Street during that time until she was asked to leave."

"Why was she asked to leave?"

"According to the police report," she paused as she read the report, "her son accused Father O'Donnell of molesting him for five years. Terry Carson, now aged," she paused to do the math in her head, "forty-seven had told his mother about the incident with him. Her response to her son was just sick. She told him that he was going to burn in hell for lying about a man of God."

"I'd be angry, too, if my mother said that to me," Daniels

said.

"But that's not the end of it. He continued talking about it to other members of the congregation. When he refused to stop, she was asked to leave the church and never come back."

"Were any charges filed against Father O'Donnell?" Sam asked.

"No. And there wasn't any physical evidence that could verify Terry's claims. It boiled down to his word against the Father's. The police did an investigation, but let's face it. That was the 1970s. Most people didn't take those kinds of allegations seriously. And the word of a priest versus the word of a kid?"

"Alright. Do we know if Terry Carson had any connection to Marcia Albright or Bryant Anderson?"

As Nina began typing again, Junior went to his computer and began typing also. After a few moments, Nina said, "Here it is. The 1983 Modesto High School registry shows Marcia Albright was a freshman, and both Bryant Anderson and Terry Carson were sophomores."

"Does it say where Pricilla Carson and her son lived before Modesto?" Sam asked.

"I've got that," Junior said. "You're going to love this. Pricilla Carson divorced Maxwell Colton in 1971. Court documents show that he had been physically abusive to both her and Terry. Hospital records entered into evidence revealed that Terry had a broken nose and several bruises and lacerations on the face consistent with physical abuse, all by the time he was three. The couple separated in December of 1970. After the divorce, Pricilla and Terry moved in with her mother in Fresno. In September of 1976, Terry Carson entered third grade. His teacher was…"

"Henry Jackson. With Nathan Carter as his classmate."

"School records from Fresno indicate that young Terry was being bullied by Nathan, almost from the beginning of the school year. The first report was filled during the last week of September. By January of 1977 there were eight complaints to the principal's office. The final one involved Terry receiving a broken arm."

"Didn't Mister Jackson try to intervene?" Jennifer asked.

"Several of the complaints allege that he encouraged Nathan's behavior. He is even quoted as saying to Nathan that he should 'teach that little bitch to grow up to be a man and not a sissy little baby girl.'"

"Wow. And they didn't fire him?"

"No. Much like with Father O'Donnell, it was his word against his teacher's. The man had tenure. In the '70s? Who was going to believe a kid?"

"Oh my God," Nina said.

"What?" the three detectives said in unison.

"After high school, Terry Carson got a full ride scholarship to Stanford School of Medicine. He lived at the University Lane apartments until he lost his funding. With the no money available for him, he got evicted. The plaintiff's name on the unlawful detainer was John Porter."

"Do we have any information as to why he lost his scholarship?"

"The documents listed from Stanford's Disciplinary Review Board show that Terry Carson had been referred to the Dean for disciplinary action by Professor Miles Elliot. Terry had been accused of engaging in some inappropriate conduct with one of the female cadavers."

"That's disgusting!" Junior shouted.

"How did he know what Terry had done? Did he witness the event himself?"

"No. The Professor stated to the Review Board that one of the other students reported the misconduct. The eyewitness to the misconduct was Blake Covington."

"Do we have a connection to Jane Woodman?"

"Nothing yet."

"Do we have a picture of this guy? Of Terry Carson? A driver's license? An address? Anything?"

"Not yet."

"Keep digging," Sam said.

45

SATURDAY

Michael Erikson was adjusting his tie as he walked into his kitchen. Linda Erikson was sliding the bacon onto her husband's plate when he walked into the room. "Here you go, hun," she said. She handed him the plate and he gave her a peck on the cheek.

He took the plate over to the table, sat down and asked, "Have you seen Sean this morning? Last night he asked me if I'd drop him off at the skate park on my way into work this morning."

"You work too hard," Linda said. "This case has consumed you. I haven't seen you this stressed out since the Chappell Hill murders."

"Yeah, that was a tough case. We lost two of our own, and we almost lost Darryl Powers when we went in to make the arrest. I don't think Sam would have forgiven herself if he had died that day."

"Well, I hope this case gets solved soon. You haven't taken a day off in more than two weeks now and you're gone all the time, every day. This isn't good for your health."

"It'll be over soon. I've got some vacation time accrued. Once this case is resolved, why don't we take Sean and go away for a while. Somewhere we can relax. Just the three of us. Maybe we can rent a houseboat at Lake Elsinore."

"That would be wonderful. It'll be like our trip, four years ago. Sean will be so excited! Let me go get him. You finish eating."

Michael watched his wife as she bounded out of the room. It was good for her to have something to look forward to. Hell, they all needed it. Sean was about to turn eighteen, and soon would be leaving for college. And God knows I could use a break after this case, he thought.

From upstairs he could hear his wife begin to shout, "Michael! Michael! Come quick! It's Sean! He can't breathe!"

Michael went running up the stairs and into his son's room. From the doorway he could see his wife on her knees next to their son's bed. Sean had fallen to the floor, gasping for air. His fingernails were starting to turn blue.

Michael ran over and grabbed the inhaler off of his son's desk. He tossed it to Linda, who quickly assisted Sean with two puff of the albuterol inside.

Sean's breathing didn't appear to ease. "It's not helping him," Linda said. "He's going to need a breathing treatment."

"Where's his nebulizer?" Michael asked.

"The insurance hasn't approved it yet. He's going to have to go to the hospital. Honey, call the ambulance."

"He'll never make it in time. I'll take him in my car. I can hit the emergency lights on the car and bypass traffic. I'll call ahead to the hospital."

Together they loaded their son into Captain Erikson's sedan. He kissed his wife, reassured her that Sean would be alright and pulled away from the house, lights and sirens blazing.

46

"Thomas, please come in. And close the door behind you."

"Bob, you sound serious. What's up?"

"Please just come in and sit down. And for this meeting, I think it would be best if you called me Mister McKinley."

Thomas closed the door and sat down in the offered chair. "Alright, have it your way, *Mr. McKinley*. What's going on?"

Bob took a deep sigh. "Thomas, how long have we known each other? About twenty years now, right?"

"Eighteen. What's going on? Something's up or you wouldn't have called me in on a Saturday."

"You always were a sharp one. You know that? That's part of why I offered you the job, all those years ago. You were also controversial. Edgy. We were looking for that. We were losing ground in the ratings back then, and we needed someone like you. Someone with an edge. You've had that quality about you this whole time."

"So, what are you saying?"

"I got a call from corporate last night. It seems that with

your aggressive attacks on the LAPD, it's offended some of our sponsors. Thomas, they're starting to pull out."

"How are the ratings for my show?"

"The ratings aren't the problem. Ratings don't pay your salary. Advertisers do. And right now they're not wanting to be associated with someone who, from the sound of it, is calling for outright defiance of city officials, specifically, members of the LAPD. Many of them have expressed that they don't want their products tied to someone that might be trying to incite ordinary citizens to riot."

"So get some new advertisers!"

"We're trying. But in the meantime, I need you to apologize, on air, on your show, to the police."

"No fucking way, Bob!"

"Look, I don't like saying this anymore than you like hearing it. But this comes from the top. If you don't start your show on Monday with a formal apology, it'll be your last."

Thomas got up and stormed towards the door.

"Thomas, come back here."

"Fuck you, and the horse you rode in on," he shouted as he slammed the door behind him.

By the time Thomas had made it out of the building, he was seething with rage. How dare they demand such a thing of him? Apologize to the police? Where was the loyalty to your people, Bob? Why didn't you tell corporate where they could stick it, Bob?

Thomas was livid as he stepped into the street. So much so, that he failed to notice that the light of the crosswalk had turned red. The driver of the approaching silver Honda looked up sufficiently to see the light had turned green, but was too busy trying to read a text to see the man that stepped off of the street corner into her path. Neither had seen the other until it was too late.

47

"Sam, come here a second," Jennifer said.

"What have you got?"

"I found something you're going to want to see. I managed to get a digital copy of the Modesto High School's yearbook for both 1983 and 1984. Look at this picture and read the caption."

Sam looked over Jennifer's shoulder and saw a picture of two teenagers in formal attire dancing. The picture was dark and hazy and the faces were blurred. "Terry Carson and Marcia Albright, couple most likely to stay together," the caption read.

"But in the 1984 yearbook," Jennifer said, opening up the book for Sam, "look at this picture and caption."

The picture was of a young football player arm in arm with a cheerleader. "Bryant Anderson (shown with his girlfriend Marcia Albright) after scoring the winning touchdown," it said.

"Son of a bitch!" Sam said. "There's the connection."

"But that's not all," Jennifer said. "Take a look at the school picture for Terry Carson. Does he look like anyone you know?"

Sam looked at the page she was being shown. At Jennifer's fingertip was the name Terry Carson. Above the printed name was the picture of a much younger, Thomas Collins.

Nina Sheppard added, "And when I looked deeper into it, Thomas Collins didn't exist until after Terry Carson was expelled from Stanford. He was a persona created for the radio."

"And he was engaged to Jane Woodman," Junior added. "Maybe she somehow found out who he really was."

"Put an APB out on Terry Carson, aka Thomas Collins," Sam said. "I want him in custody today." She picked up her phone and started dialing.

"What are you doing?" Junior asked.

"I'm calling Captain Erikson. He's going to want to know what we've found. I'm surprised that he's not here already." His phone rang once, but quickly went to voicemail. "That's weird," she said and dialed the number again.

"Sam, I've got Sean at the hospital emergency room. Is this important?"

"We know who the killer is. We've identified him and his motive. We can link him to all twelve of the victims."

"Good work. What do you need from me?"

"I hate to ask you to come down here, with Sean being in the hospital, but we need to get a warrant to search his house. We've got an APB out on him, but I want to get any evidence we can before he gets rid of it."

Sam could hear Erikson cover up his phone. "Sean, are you going to be okay if I go down to the station and handle this?" she could hear him ask his son.

Sean's response was muffled but she could make out his response. "Yeah dad, I'll be okay. I'm breathing a whole lot better. Besides, the doctor said I'd be here for a few more hours anyway."

The clear voice of Captain Erikson returned to the phone. "Sam, I'll be right down. By the time you get to his house, you'll have that warrant."

She hung up the phone and looked at her expecting team. She finally realized that fact. This was her team. "Let's get moving," she said with pride. "We've got a sick, son of a bitch to arrest. Let's go get him."

48

"I'm sure you do feel fine, Mister Collins," Patrick Benson said. "But that's a nasty bump on your head. You were unconscious for more than ten minutes after you were hit by that car. You're lucky she was slowing down to make that turn or you could've been hurt much worse. We just want to observe you for a little while. The doctor will be in soon enough. As soon as he sees you, I can get you started on some medicine for your pain."

"I don't have time for this," he shouted as his nurse walked out. To the room at large he said, "I hate hospitals."

"I know what you mean," said a voice from behind the shared curtain where the room's other occupant was. "From the way the nurse was talking, it sounds like you got hit by a car."

"Apparently I was. I don't remember anything after stepping out into the street. What are you in here for?" he asked.

Sean Erikson pulled back the curtain separating the two. "Severe asthma attack. Los Angeles is probably the worst place in the world I could live with my asthma. I usually can keep it under control with my emergency inhaler, but this morning it was too bad."

"Sorry to hear that kid." His world started to swoon. "You

know, on second thought, I think I will lay back for a few."

"Do you mind if I turn the television on?" Sean asked.

"Knock yourself out kid." He laid back and put his hand above his eyes, squeezing his forehead.

Sean turned the shared television set on and turned the sound down as low as he possibly could, while still being able to hear it. The first channel was an infomercial. The next channel was a movie from the eighties. When he turned the television to the next channel, he looked into the face of his father.

"…pleased to announce that we have identified a person of interest in the recent series of homicides that began two weeks ago. Terry Carson, also known as Thomas Collins is being sought in connection with the deaths of Blake Covington, Jane Woodman and Miles Elliot, as well as several other individuals throughout Northern and Southern California. If you see this man, do not attempt to confront him. He is considered armed and dangerous…"

Sean was surprised when his roommate sat up so quickly at the mention of the name Terry Carson. He was also surprised how this man that was just laying down, clearly in pain, had continued to sit up, eyes glued to the television, mouth gaping, for the remainder of the announcement by his father; until the picture was shown.

"This is a picture of Terry Carson, aka Thomas Collins."

The remainder of his father's speech was drowned out. As the picture was flashed onto the screen, Sean look from the television to the man in the bed next to him. He looked back from the man to the television, his mouth gaping open. Once again, he looked from the television to the man he was sharing a room with. Then he began screaming.

"Help! Somebody help! Help!"

Patrick came rushing in. "You need to be quiet, young man. You'll disturb the other patients."

"But he's the killer. You've got to call my father. You've got to get me out of here!"

The nurse looked at Thomas and said, "Do you know what he's talking about?"

"I don't have the faintest idea," he said.

"Help!" Sean cried out. "Call security!" He started wheezing again.

"Sean, calm down. You're going to trigger another asthma attack. Relax and lay back. The medicine the doctor gave you can sometimes make you anxious. He prescribed some anti-anxiety medication for you…"

"I'm… not… having… anxiety," Sean wheezed.

"Look, if this is going to be a problem, I'll just leave," Thomas said.

"No, lay back down. The doctor needs to take a look at you. We've got to make sure you're okay after an accident like that. I don't want anyone dying on my watch." He attached the tubes of the oxygen mask to the supply line in the wall. Then he put the mask over Sean's face and said, "Just take some nice deep breaths, and I'll be right back with your medication."

"I... don't... need..." Sean began, only to be interrupted by the intercom system.

"We have a code blue in bed four A. Code blue in four A," it said.

"Shit," Patrick said. "That's two rooms away. Calm down. You'll be fine. I'll be right back with your medicine." Then he ran out of the room.

After several minutes of working on the patient in room four A, Patrick took a second to gather his thoughts. He looked over the list of his patients and saw the name Sean Erikson.

That's right, he thought. I need to get him his anti-anxiety medication. At least he sounds like he's calmed down. He's not screaming anymore.

He went over to the medicine cart, punched in his code and the drawer containing the medications popped open. He took out the vial, plunged the needle into the lid, and filled the syringe with the contents. He walked back into the room and said, "Now isn't that better? Like I said before, when you lay back and..."

Patrick looked up as his words stopped dead in his mouth. In the bed nearer to the door lay Sean's body, covered with stab wounds to the chest. A pillow lay over his face. The other bed was empty.

49

Sam and Junior pulled up in front of Thomas' home. Sheppard and Daniels flanked them, along with five patrol cars.

As they exited the vehicle, Sam began barking orders. "You two," she pointed to the uniformed officers. "Go around back. You, you and you, set up eyes and ears here. Look for anyone on a roof, behind a tree…"

"Sam," Jennifer said.

"He's not going to get the jump on us."

"Sam," Jennifer said again.

"What?" Sam barked.

"This isn't Chappell Hill. Darryl's not here. You don't have to…"

Sam glared ice at Daniels. "You think I don't know that? This isn't the time or place to bring that up. But let me assure you, I know I'm here in the present and now, not living in the past." She walked up to the door and kicked it open. "Thomas Collins! Terry Carson! We have a warrant for your arrest!"

They cleared the house room by room. There was no

evidence to be seen that could link him to the crimes. After a few minutes, Junior called out, "Hey Detective! I've got a locked door here."

Sam walked up and kicked hard. The door flew open. She reached out and flicked the light switch that lit the entire flight of stairs down into the garage. Weapons drawn, together, they started down the steps.

"Do you smell something?" Junior asked.

"Yeah, I do."

"What do you think it is?" he whispered.

Embalming fluid is what it smells like, she thought. "I don't know," she said.

At the bottom of the stairs was another light switch. Junior flicked it on. When their eyes had adjusted to the light Sam said, "Gotcha you son of a bitch." Junior turned and began retching.

In the garage, in the space closest to them, was the blue Bugatti that had once been driven by Blake Covington. On the back wall of the garage, were the surgical tools that would be necessary to perform a vivisection. The tools were covered in blood.

Sam pulled out her cell phone to dial up the captain. When he answered, Sam blurted out, "We've got the evidence. We've nailed him!"

"That's good, Sam," he said softly. It sounded like he was crying.

"Sir, did you hear me? I said we can prove he did it."

"I heard you, Sam. Sean's dead. He killed him. He killed my boy! Terry Carson killed my only son!" the captain said, and he dissolved into tears.

50

Over one hundred officers were assembled when Sam began speaking.

"We've identified the suspect in the murder of thirteen people, including Captain Erikson's son, as Terry Collins, aka Thomas Collins. He was last seen leaving the hospital where he killed the Captain's son. We've secured his home and frozen his assets. We've passed his photo to the TSA agents at all local airports, as well as bus and train stations. His photo has been broadcast on all of the major networks in Los Angeles. He will not get away.

"And that's what makes him dangerous. We're boxing him in. He's without friends and without money. He has no known means of transportation." She pulled up a map of the city near the hospital. "That's why we're focusing our efforts on this area here," she motioned with the laser pointer to an area on the map. "He is to be considered armed and dangerous. Take whatever means are necessary to bring him down."

The room began to empty as officer after officer began the hunt for Terry Carson/Thomas Collins.

"I can't believe he had the nerve to go after the captain's son," Nina said.

"And in the hospital, no less," Jennifer added.

"He didn't have a choice, really," Junior said.

"And just what is that supposed to mean?" Sam demanded.

"I'm not trying to be offensive or inconsiderate of anyone's feelings here. But you yourself said it. He's at his most dangerous point right now. The captain's son somehow was able to identify him. He couldn't let him live."

"So let's get that son of a bitch," Nina said.

Sam's desk phone began ringing. She walked over and picked it up. "Detective Franklin," she said.

"Detective, this is Officer Jackson. We just got a call on the tip line from someone that said they just saw your guy cutting through the old cemetery down by the marina."

"That's right in the heart of our search area. Get officers down there now. Surround the place but do not engage. We'll be there in five minutes."

"We've got him," Sam said, hanging up the phone. "He's cutting through the old cemetery by the marina. If he makes it there and gets on board one of those boats, he'll be gone for good. Let's go."

51

When Sam arrived at the cemetery, she was approached by a familiar face. "I'm surprised to see you here," she said to Officer Davis.

"Yes, Detective. And I won't be making that kind of mistake again," he said, glaring at Junior.

"Give me an update," Sam ordered.

"We arrived from the west, and we spotted the suspect heading towards us. We ordered him to stop, but he turned and ran. Fortunately, when the call came through, several other patrolling officers showed up from the north and blocked his escape. He's cornered. We have him surrounded."

Sam pulled out her gun. "Show me where the coward's hiding."

As they approached Thomas, Sam began to understand how they had managed to corner him while only surrounding him in a half circle. On the far side of the graves was a fifteen foot high masonry wall that fenced off the south and east sides of the property. To the west and to the north ten officers were crouched behind tombstones, each one with their gun trained on Thomas Collins. He was kneeling down in front of a tombstone with his back to them all.

"Thomas Collins! This is Samantha Franklin, LAPD. You are under arrest for the murders of Blake Covington, Jane Woodman, Miles Elliot and Sean Erikson. Put your hands up where I can see them and turn around slowly!"

"You don't understand," he shouted from the kneeling position with his back towards her. "You just don't get it."

"What is it that you think I don't get? Why you killed Blake? Or the others?"

"They all deserved what they got. Blake Covington was a spoiled rich brat. His father gave him everything. He hated me and lied about me. He and Professor Elliot conspired to get me kicked out of med school."

"I know all about that. And the things the others did, too, Thomas."

"No, you have no idea how much they deserved what they got. And how much more they deserved."

"You can tell me all about it when we get back to the station. You can tell me everything. But right now, you need to give yourself up."

"There's no way I'll get a fair trial. Not here. Not now."

Sam could see that he was trying to build up his nerve to do the ultimate of stupid things. "Don't talk like that, Thomas. I promise you, here and now, that you will get a fair trial. You have to trust me on this. Let me help you. This isn't how you want to be remembered."

"It's too late. This will be my legacy."

Thomas jumped to his feet and spun around. He reached his hand into his pocket. From behind Sam, someone yelled, "Gun!" Fourteen officers fired their weapons into Thomas Collins' head and chest.

EPILOGUE

The first few days after the take down of Thomas Collins aka Terry Carson were a blur for Sam. After the debriefing, and the investigation by internal affairs, Sam was awarded the Medal of Valor. She and the other members of her team were also awarded the Police Star.

A week after his death, they laid to rest Sean Erikson. His autopsy report showed that he had been stabbed twenty-seven times in the chest. In one of the stab wounds, Jack Adams had found the missing Hamate bone of Miles Elliot.

The Friday, three weeks after the funeral, Captain Erikson called Sam into his office.

"How are you and Linda holding up?" she asked.

"It's been hard. I keep expecting him to come through the door, asking for help with his homework, things like that. Linda's been inconsolable. Sam, how do you manage?"

"You never stop missing them. But it does get easier. I threw myself into my work. This job saved me."

"We're going to go away for a while. I have about six weeks accrued. I think we need some time away."

"That's good, sir. Everyone works through the grief

process at a different pace. Take the time you need. Then come back when you're ready."

"Is that your Psychology training coming out?"

"No, sir. It's my life experience."

"So did you and Leslie ever work out your differences?"

"My sister? No. She never forgave me after mom and dad died. I haven't spoken to her in six years."

"Maybe you should reach out to her before it's too late. Just a thought."

"Maybe," she said as she turned to leave. "I might do that."

When Sam arrived home that evening, she found a package waiting for her. That's odd, she thought. I'm not expecting anything.

She picked up the package and carried it inside. She took it to her dining room table and sat down to open it. There was no return address on it, but the postage indicated that it had been sent to her from China.

Her curiosity peaked, she opened it up to find an old photo album. It looked like the one her father had once had from when he was younger. Opening the red vinyl cover revealed the black interior pages, complete with the plastic corners where you could insert the pictures. She looked on the inside cover and her heart leapt at the familiar name written there. *Property of Jeffery Franklin* , it read.

Leslie! Leslie was reaching out to her! She had gone into the house in Newark and got dad's old photo album. Maybe she was piecing together photos from their childhood. She quickly turned the page and her heart dropped.

On the first page, she saw pictures of a crime scene. They weren't fresh and new like you would expect from a digital camera. These were clearly from a 35mm camera, and from many, many years ago. There was something else about the pictures. They almost looked like crime scene photos the police would take, but these were taken before any police had arrived.

On the second page were more of the same kinds of pictures. This continued on for several pages before a newspaper article shouted the headline, "Parkside Strangler Killed in Shootout with Police." It was dated June 7, 1981.

This was followed by another series of older photos leading to the newspaper article whose headline read, "Mission Valley Butcher Cornered and Killed." December 12, 1983 was the date on that one.

When the twenty-seventh series of murders began, the first picture on the page was the photo of Max Colton's murder scene. This was followed by one of each of Terry Carson's victims up to and including Sean Erikson.

Sam turned the page past Sean's pictures to find the cut out from each victim's skin taped to the pages: "**LOOK WHAT I CAN DO**"; "**THOSE WHO CAN'T TEACH**"; "**NOW ITS PERSONAL SAMANTHA**."

She turned the page one last time and read the hand

written note.

Are you sure this is over, Samantha?

Pete Alexander

August 15, 2015

About the Author

Pete Alexander was born in Southern California, USA, in 1970. His family moved frequently. He spent equal time growing up in urban Southern California and rural Northern California. He loves to travel and to spend time with his family and friends. He loves to play music and had thought of starting a band in the early 1990s.

Pete began writing at the age of eight. Very little of his work ever saw the light of day. This book, Tortured Souls, includes some of his earlier work. For instance, the song that begins chapter two, he wrote in 1998. The band that performs that song is what he had intended to call his band.

Pete currently lives in Long Beach, California with his wife and two children.

Coming Soon

Past Sins

The Second

Samantha Franklin Novel

Catching up with you in 2016